Elsie's Troubled Times

Elsie's Troubled Times

BOOK SIX

of the
Elsie Dinsmore:
A Life of Faith
Series

Based on the beloved books by
Martha Finley

MCP
Mission City Press
Franklin, Tennessee

Book Six of the *Elsie Dinsmore: A Life of Faith* Series

Elsie's Troubled Times
Copyright © 2000, Mission City Press, Inc. All Rights Reserved.

Published by Mission City Press, Inc.

This book is based on the *Elsie Dinsmore* books written by Martha Finley and first published in 1868 by Dodd, Mead & Company.

Cover & Interior Design: Richmond & Williams, Nashville, Tennessee
Cover Photography: Michelle Grisco Photography, Franklin, Tennessee
Typesetting: BookSetters, White House, Tennessee

Elsie Dinsmore: A Life of Faith is a trademark of Mission City Press, Inc.

For more information, write to Mission City Press at P.O. Box 681913, Franklin, Tennessee 37068-1913, or visit our Web Site at

www.Elsie–Dinsmore.com

Library of Congress Catalog Card Number: 99-65159
Finley, Martha
    Elsie's Troubled Times
    Book Six of the *Elsie Dinsmore: A Life of Faith* Series
    ISBN: 1-928749-06-2

Printed in the United States of America
2 3 4 5 6 7 8 — 06 05 04 03 02 01

DEDICATION

This book is
dedicated to
the memory of
MARTHA FINLEY

May the rich legacy of
pure and simple devotion to Christ
that she introduced through
Elsie Dinsmore in 1868
live on in our day and
in generations to come.

— FOREWORD —

*I*n the previous book of the *Elsie Dinsmore: A Life of Faith* series, Elsie found her true love and married him. Now, she is about to begin a new life as wife and mistress of her own home. There seem to be few clouds on her horizon as she and her husband return from their honeymoon, but life is never so simple or easy. Elsie, like everyone else in the United States at the end of the 1850s, will soon become caught up in one of the darkest periods of American history—the Civil War. No one who is dear to Elsie will be unaffected by the events of this long and costly struggle.

When Martha Finley began creating her Elsie Dinsmore books in the 1860s, the Civil War was still very fresh in the minds of all her countrymen. Even young readers had fathers, grandfathers, uncles, and brothers who had fought in the war. The fortunate survivors, many left with serious wounds and lifelong disabilities, were a constant reminder of the sorrow and grief that occurs when a country is divided and men take up arms against one another. As she wrote the story of Elsie and her loved ones during the war, Miss Finley made it her goal "to be as impartial as if writing history" and through her writing "to make the very thought of a renewal of the awful strife *utterly abhorrent* to every lover of humanity, and especially of this, our own dear native land."

Miss Finley herself was a loyal Unionist; she believed in the United States as a single nation. "Are we not one people," she asked, "speaking the same language; worshipping the one and true living God; having a common history, a common ancestry; and united by the tenderest ties of blood?" It was her hope and prayer that the people of the nation should put aside all feelings of bitterness and be reunited "in love, harmony, and mutual helpfulness."

In adapting *Elsie's Troubled Times*, every effort has been made to preserve Miss Finley's commitment to fairness in presenting both sides of the conflict: the Union and the Southern Confederacy. The story is seen through Elsie's eyes; it is fiction but also a reflection of the personal experiences and trials endured by real people, both Northern and Southern, during the period leading up to the war and in the four years of the Civil War.

Mission City Press is pleased to carry on Miss Finley's message of faith, hope, and Christian love in *Elsie's Troubled Times* and in all the books of the *Elsie Dinsmore: A Life of Faith* series.

✍ THE AMERICAN CIVIL WAR ✍

A civil war is an armed conflict waged between citizens of the same country. Many nations have experienced the devastation of civil war throughout history, and today in various parts of the world, people of opposing viewpoints are fighting civil wars for control of their countries. Civil wars occur when people feel that they cannot compromise on their beliefs or that they are being abused by another section of their society, and when political efforts to resolve deeply held differences fail.

The United States experienced its failure to find compromise in the decades prior to April 1861. What followed was four years of war (1861-1865) which cost the nation more lives than any other conflict except the Second World War. Although exact numbers are not possible to determine, at least 650,000 Americans on both sides died or were wounded during the fighting.

Foreword

How did the nation get to the point where people were willing to put aside the closest ties of family and friendship and to wage war against their fellow citizens?

Many factors can be cited as causes of the Civil War, but two were predominant: the practice of slavery in the Southern states and the conflict over the rights and powers of the individual American states versus the rights and powers of the United States as a whole. By the end of the 1850s, many people in the South were ready to separate their states from the Union—to secede—in order to defend their right to govern themselves as they saw fit.

It is important to understand that the United States in the 1850s was not at all like the United States of our time. It was still a nation of small farms and small businesses. Although the North was beginning to industrialize, the nation was still dependent on agriculture, natural resources and, in large measure, on the cotton economy of the South. By 1860, cotton accounted for almost sixty percent of all American exports—goods sold outside the country. In turn, the production of cotton depended on the use of slave labor.

The Northern states had given up slave-owning principally because it was not economical. (Farms in New England and other Northern states tended to be small, seasonal, and less productive than in the South, so supporting slaves was too expensive.) But by 1860, there were approximately 3.5 million slaves in the Southern states—more than a third of the total population of that region.

The North was changing quickly as the 1850s came to a close. Its cities were growing; its transportation systems, roads and railways were expanding; its new manufacturing industries were becoming established. Immigrants, primarily from Europe, were flooding into the North on their way to the rich but untamed territories of the West. These were exciting, dynamic times in the North, and Northerners looked to the federal government in Washington for help in making their growth profitable.

But the South was barely changed. Other than New Orleans, its major cities were little more than sleepy rural towns. Its transportation systems were poor and undeveloped, and factories were virtually non-existent. The South sought little from the federal government and feared that Northern demands (such as high taxes on goods imported from other countries) would damage the Southern economy. Southerners also wanted to expand their cotton production into the new states of the West, and to take slavery into these states. During the decades prior to the Civil War, Southern leaders had become increasingly fearful that the fast-growing North would gain control of the federal government.

Most of the quarrels between North and South might well have been worked out peacefully in the political arena. But as Civil War historian Bruce Catton noted, "Slavery poisoned the whole situation. It was the issue that could not be compromised, the issue that made men so angry they did not want to compromise."*

There had been attempts to come to terms on slavery. For example, the Missouri Compromise of 1820 allowed Missouri to be admitted to the Union as a slave state, but stipulated that no new states formed above the southern border of Missouri would be admitted as slave states. Henry Clay's Compromise of 1850 made California a free state and abolished slavery in the District of Columbia but also enacted strict new fugitive slave laws. In 1854, Congress passed the Kansas-Nebraska Act that formalized the concept of "popular sovereignty," or allowing every new state that entered the Union to make its own choice to be free or to permit slavery. As a result, the territory of Kansas became an early battleground in the fight between anti-slavery and pro-slavery forces. As each "compromise" was tried and failed, extremists on both sides grew louder and more

Foreword

fierce, all but silencing the moderates who sought reasonable solutions.

In 1857, the Supreme Court of the United States handed down a decision that had the same effect as gasoline thrown on a burning fire. In the Dred Scott case, the highest court in the land declared that Negroes could not be citizens of any state or the nation and that the institution of slavery was protected by the U.S. Constitution. Attempts to ban slavery from any new state were therefore illegal. The federal government under President James Buchanan (a Pennsylvanian who nevertheless sympathized with the South) was paralyzed—incapable of taking any serious action amid so much conflict.

Yet it was the act of one individual—an abolitionist named John Brown who had already led a murderous attack on Southern settlers in Kansas—that seemed to set the country on a direct path to war. On October 16, 1859, John Brown and his followers attacked the United States arsenal at Harper's Ferry, Virginia. Brown planned to seize the guns and other weapons in the arsenal, escape to the hills, and then start a massive slave rebellion. Brown's men were quickly subdued by a detachment of Marines led by an Army colonel named Robert E. Lee. (Lee, a graduate of West Point military academy and veteran of the Mexican War, would sadly side with his native Virginia when the Civil War broke out.) John Brown was tried and then hanged for treason, but his action stirred the pot of anger and fear which was brewing.

Northern extremists held Brown up as a hero of the abolitionist cause, while Southerners interpreted the Harper's Ferry raid as proof of Northern intentions to create a slave uprising that would lead all the South into a bloodbath.

When Abraham Lincoln became President of the United States after the contentious election campaign of 1860, Southerners took it as a sign that their ambitions to expand their slave economy had come to an end. Lincoln, a Republican and

xiii

a moderate, had promised that he would not interfere with slavery in the states where it was already legal, but he would oppose its spread to the new territories and states. (In 1860, the United States comprised thirty-two states. Kansas joined the Union in 1861, and West Virginia, which broke away from Virginia, entered the Union in 1863.) Lincoln did not receive a majority of the popular vote, but the national political parties, which had divided on North-South lines, were so weakened by their infighting that none could field a candidate stronger than Lincoln.

Shortly after the election, the legislature of South Carolina — acting on what it believed to be every state's right to leave the Union — voted for secession, or separation. Six more Southern states (Mississippi, Florida, Alabama, Georgia, Louisiana, and Texas) soon followed South Carolina and formed themselves into an independent nation which they called the Confederate States of America.**

President James Buchanan, in his last weeks in office, denied that the Southern states had a right to secede, yet he also held that the federal government had no right to use force against the secessionist states. Inside the government and through private efforts, the nation's leaders continued to search for a compromise that would restore the Union and appease the South. But actions that would lead to full-scale war were already under way.

The Confederacy had taken control of a number of federal forts and other facilities and refused to pay taxes and duties to the U.S. government. In January 1861, President Buchanan sent an unarmed merchant ship to carry soldiers and ammunition to Fort Sumter, a federal garrison in the harbor of Charleston, South Carolina. The Southerners fired at the ship, and it turned away. The Union, still trying to avoid open battle, left the small garrison of soldiers at Fort Sumter to fend for themselves.

When Lincoln came to office, he continued this policy regarding Fort Sumter; he did not want the Union to be the aggressor if a battle was waged. But sympathies in the North began to focus on the beleaguered men in the fort. It had

become a symbol of the Union. In the first week of April, Lincoln notified the governor of South Carolina that reinforcements were being sent to Fort Sumter; however, this attempt to supply the fort would be peaceful. But the new president of the Confederacy, Jefferson Davis, ordered that Fort Sumter be taken. Under the command of General P. G. T. Beauregard, the bombardment of Fort Sumter began on April 12. After two days of shelling, which reduced much of the fort to rubble, the Union commander, Major Robert Anderson, was forced to surrender. His band of tired and hungry soldiers was allowed to leave and return homeward, and the flag of the Union was hauled down.

Although efforts at settlement were still being made, the first shots of war had been fired. The battle lines had been drawn at Fort Sumter, and there was no turning back.

In April of 1861, most people believed that the conflict would not last long—a few months at most. On both sides, soldiers marched off with confidence, cheered on by their families and friends. In the South, the fever for battle infected almost everyone*** despite the fact that the South was at a disadvantage in almost every respect. The total population of the Confederate states was less than half the population of the Union states. (During the war, the South had fewer than a million men under arms, compared to the North's more than 2 million troops.) The South's ability to supply its armies with food, clothing, guns and ammunition was very limited. It had little manufacturing capability; its road, railway, and communications systems were minimal, and the North controlled most of the nation's naval shipping. The Confederates printed their own money, but it was worthless outside their borders. The South counted on aid from England and Europe, but that never came.

Yet in the face of such overwhelming odds, Southerners believed that the superiority of their fighting forces and their generals would win the day. The South would be fighting a

defensive war to protect and secure its own territory, and war generally favors an army fighting on its own ground. It was true that the Confederacy had an extraordinary complement of skilled military leaders—many of them, like Lee and the brilliant Thomas J. "Stonewall" Jackson, educated at West Point. But even the best generals and bravest soldiers could not, in the long run, compensate for the region's poverty of resources and lack of outside allies. And the South also made the mistake of underestimating the ability and determination of their Northern foes.

Almost exactly four years after the surrender of Fort Sumter, America's bloodiest and most destructive war came to its end with the Confederate surrender at Appomattox Court House on April 9, 1865. The principle that the United States is an unbreakable union of states had triumphed, and the end of slavery had been achieved—with the deaths of hundreds of thousands of men and boys and the devastation of the Southern social and economic order.

When President Lincoln was inaugurated for his second term in March of 1865, he struggled to find a rational explanation for the war. Yet despite his political skill and human wisdom, Lincoln turned to God for direction. Both sides of the conflict, Lincoln said, "read the same Bible and pray to the same God, and each invokes His aid against the other . . . . The prayers of both could not be answered; that of neither has been answered fully. The Almighty has His own purposes."

Within six weeks of this speech, the Civil War was ended, Lincoln was dead, and a divided nation was left to mourn its lost men, stitch up its wounds, and begin the work of healing itself.

---

* *The American Heritage Picture History of The Civil War*, written by Pulitzer Prize-winning historian Bruce Catton and first published by the American Heritage Publishing Company in 1960, remains one of the most thorough, balanced, and readable books

on the causes and the conduct of the war. But there are many excellent books on the subject, including a number written specifically for young readers.

** By the summer of 1861, the Confederate States of America also included Virginia, Arkansas, Tennessee, and North Carolina for a total of eleven states. Four slave states remained in the Union: Maryland, Delaware, Missouri, and Kentucky, which, with West Virginia, are often called the "border states." The Union, or free, states were Maine, Vermont, New Hampshire, Massachusetts, Connecticut, New York, Rhode Island, New Jersey, Pennsylvania, Ohio, Indiana, Illinois, Michigan, Wisconsin, Minnesota, Kansas, Oregon, and California.

*** Not all loyalties could be simply divided by North and South. Eastern Tennessee, for example, was not a slave-owning area and had little sympathy for secession; unsuccessful efforts were made to separate this area from the rest of the state before Tennessee joined the Confederacy in 1861. Likewise the western portion of Virginia opposed secession; this region separated from Virginia in 1861 and was admitted to the Union as the state of West Virginia in 1863. Missouri and Kentucky, on the other hand, did not secede, but their citizens were divided; both states refused President Lincoln's original call for troops, and many Kentuckians fought for the Confederacy when their state became a battleground.

Elsie's Troubled Times

KEY EVENTS AND BATTLES
OF THE CIVIL WAR

December, 1860	South Carolina secedes from the Union.
February, 1861	The Confederate States of America is formed; Jefferson Davis of Mississippi becomes its president.
March 4, 1861	Abraham Lincoln of Illinois is inaugurated as President of the United States.
April 14, 1861	Union troops surrender Fort Sumter in South Carolina.
June, 1861	Confederate capital established in Richmond, Virginia.
July 21, 1861	First Battle of Bull Run, Manassas Junction, Virginia; Union troops retreat to Washington.
April 6–7, 1862	Battle of Shiloh, Pittsburg Landing, Tennessee; Union victory opens door to the Deep South.
April 24–25, 1862	Union capture of New Orleans blocks mouth of the Mississippi River.
June 26–July 1, 1862	Seven Days Battle (Mechanicsville, Gaines' Mill, Savage's Station, Frayser's Farm, Malvern Hill, Maryland); General Lee's Army of Northern Virginia stops Union advance on Richmond.
August 29–30, 1862	Second Battle of Bull Run; Confederate victory in Virginia.
September 17, 1862	Battle of Antietam, Sharpsburg, Maryland; Union stops first Confederate attempt to advance northward.

Key Events and Battles of the Civil War

December 13, 1862	Battle of Fredericksburg, Virginia; Union again fails in drive to take Richmond.
December 31, 1862–January 2, 1863	Battle of Stones River at Murfreesboro, Tennessee; Confederates defeated in Union campaign to oust them from Tennessee.
January 1, 1863	President Lincoln issues final version of the Emancipation Proclamation giving freedom to all slaves in the seceded states of the Confederacy.
May 1–4, 1863	Battle of Chancellorsville, Virginia; Lee again stops Union advance on Richmond.
July 1–3, 1863	Battle of Gettysburg, Pennsylvania; some of the war's most horrific fighting; Confederates fail in northward advance.
July 4, 1863	Confederates surrender Vicksburg, Mississippi, after long siege, giving the Union control of the Mississippi River.
September 19–20, 1863	Battle of Chickamauga in north Georgia; Confederates briefly halt Union move into Georgia.
November 23–25, 1863	Battles at Chattanooga, Tennessee; General Grant's victory leads to invasion of Georgia.
May, 1864	Battles of The Wilderness and Spotsylvania in Virginia; Lee holds back Union advance on Richmond.
September 2, 1864	Atlanta, Georgia, captured; Union forces under General Sherman begin long march to the sea.
September, 1864	Union gains control of the Shenandoah Valley.

Elsie's Troubled Times

December 15, 1864	Battle of Nashville, Tennessee; Confederates defeated in last attempt to gain the offensive in the west.
March 4, 1865	President Lincoln's second inauguration.
April 2, 1865	Confederate defense lines are finally broken at Petersburg, Virginia; Union troops enter Richmond the next day.
April 9, 1865	General Lee surrenders his Army of Northern Virginia to General Grant at Appomattox Court House in Virginia; war is ended.
April 14, 1865	President Lincoln is assassinated at Ford's Theater in Washington, D.C.

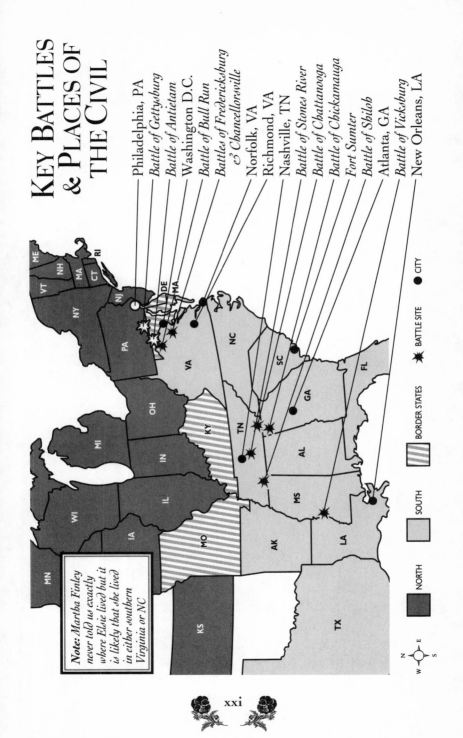

KEY BATTLES & PLACES OF THE CIVIL

Philadelphia, PA
Battle of Gettysburg
Battle of Antietam
Washington D.C.
Battle of Bull Run
Battles of Fredericksburg & Chancellorsville
Norfolk, VA
Richmond, VA
Nashville, TN
Battle of Stones River
Battle of Chattanooga
Battle of Chickamauga
Fort Sumter
Battle of Shiloh
Atlanta, GA
Battle of Vicksburg
New Orleans, LA

Note: *Martha Finley never told us exactly where Elsie lived but it is likely that she lived in either southern Virginia or NC*

* BATTLE SITE   ● CITY

NORTH   SOUTH   BORDER STATES

xxi

DINSMORE FAMILY TREE

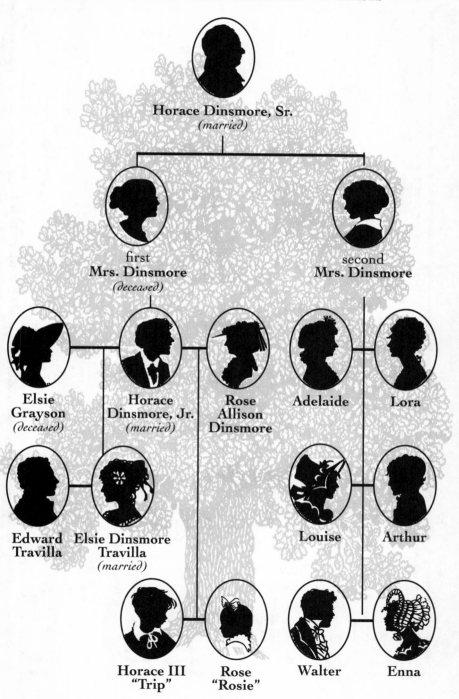

Horace Dinsmore, Sr.
(married)

first
Mrs. Dinsmore
(deceased)

second
Mrs. Dinsmore

Elsie
Grayson
(deceased)

Horace
Dinsmore, Jr.
(married)

Rose
Allison
Dinsmore

Adelaide

Lora

Edward
Travilla

Elsie Dinsmore
Travilla
(married)

Louise

Arthur

Horace III
"Trip"

Rose
"Rosie"

Walter

Enna

SETTING

*T*he story begins early in 1857 in the southern United States (the "Old South").

CHARACTERS

Elsie Dinsmore Travilla—The oldest child of Horace Dinsmore, Jr., Elsie has recently wed **Edward Travilla** of Ion plantation.

Horace Dinsmore, Jr. and Rose Allison Dinsmore—The master of The Oaks plantation and his second wife. Their children are **Horace Dinsmore, III** ("Trip"), age 11, and **Rose Dinsmore** ("Rosie"), age 3.

Mr. and Mrs. Horace Dinsmore, Sr., of Roselands plantation—Elsie's grandfather and his second wife. Their grown children are **Adelaide** (Mrs. Edward Allison), **Lora** (Mrs. Charles Howard), **Louise** (Mrs. Winston Conley of Kentucky), **Arthur**, **Walter**, and **Enna** (Mrs. Richard Percival).

Mrs. Eugenia Travilla of Ion Plantation—Edward's elderly mother.

Mr. and Mrs. Allison of Philadelphia—A wealthy merchant and his wife who are the parents of Rose Dinsmore. Their other children are **Edward** (husband of Adelaide Dinsmore), **Richard**, **Daniel**, **Sophie** (Mrs. Harry Carrington), **Fred**, **May**, and **Daisy**.

Mrs. Mary Murray of Scotland—A devout Scots Presbyterian, the widowed Mrs. Murray was once Elsie's caretaker. She lives in Edinburgh and is cared for by her nieces, **Eliza** (Mrs. MacDoogal) and **Katherine** (Mrs. Randall).

Wealthy Stanhope of Lansdale, Ohio — Horace Dinsmore, Jr.'s elderly aunt.

Harry Duncan of Ohio — Aunt Wealthy's favorite nephew.

✑ Servants ✑

Aunt Chloe — Elsie's nursemaid and personal companion.

Old Joe — An elderly slave and Chloe's husband.

Dinah — Chloe and Joe's granddaughter, now a maid at Ion.

Lavinia — Mrs. Travilla's long-time cook and housekeeper at Ion.

Becky — Mrs. Murray's devoted Scots housekeeper.

Mrs. Dowd — An English cook.

✑ Others ✑

Dr. Barton — The Dinsmores' family doctor and trusted friend.

Lucy Carrington (Mrs. Phillip Ross) — Elsie's childhood friend, she lives in New York with her husband and children.

Harry Carrington — Husband of Sophie Allison. They live at Ashlands plantation with his parents.

Lottie King — Elsie's friend from Lansdale, Lottie attends college in Vermont.

Dr. King — Lottie's father; a physician and surgeon.

Mr. Mason — The chaplain at Viamede, Elsie's sugar plantation in Louisiana.

Mr. Spriggs — A New Englander and the overseer of Viamede.

Joshua McFee and Mrs. McFee — An experienced plantation manager and his wife.

CHAPTER

Home
to Ion

*"A wife of noble character who can
find? She watches over the affairs
of her household and does not
eat the bread of idleness."*

PROVERBS 31:10, 27

Home to Ion

*E*lsie and Edward's return from their honeymoon was greeted with the greatest excitement at The Oaks and at Ion. They had decided to go to The Oaks first, in part because Elsie was so anxious to see her father and dear family. But Edward was also determined to tell Horace immediately of the events that had hastened their departure from Viamede and to assure him of their safety.

"So you truly believe Jackson is no longer a threat?" Horace asked. Elsie and Rose had joined the children in the playroom, and the two men were alone in the library. Edward had just completed a detailed account of Tom Jackson's attack and apparent flight to the West.

"He will be a threat to everyone he encounters until he is locked behind prison bars for the rest of his life," Edward answered. "But I do not believe he would dare return to Louisiana or here. He knows that every agent of the law has been alerted to be on watch for him. He is a vile and vengeful creature, but he is also a coward of the worst sort."

"As his sneaking attack in the night demonstrates," Horace interjected angrily.

"But his fear for his own safety is our greatest ally," Edward went on. "However much he wants revenge, he will not risk his skin again to achieve it. Remember that when wounded, he ran like a dog. No, Horace, I feel confident we have seen the last of him. You need not worry for Elsie's sake now."

"But we must be cautious," Horace said.

"Of course," Edward replied. "I shall see to it that his description is known to everyone within a hundred miles of here."

"We must know if he ever returns to this vicinity. I think it would be wise to offer a reward to anyone who spots him and reports his presence to us or the sheriff. But tell me honestly, old friend, are you as certain as you seem?"

Edward smiled and clasped Horace's shoulder firmly. "I cannot be absolutely certain of anything. But, yes, I believe that Jackson's low character will prevent him from making any further attempts to harm any of us. Your daughter — my wife — is safe now. She may begin her life at Ion in peace."

So it was not fear that brought such a wistful expression to Horace's face as Elsie and Edward entered their carriage later that day for the ride to Ion.

"You miss her already, dearest," said Rose gently as she slipped her arm around her husband.

"Am I so obvious?" he asked, watching as the carriage disappeared from sight.

"No," she said gently. "You kept your cheerful facade for Elsie, and she noticed nothing amiss. But your melancholy is natural, dear Horace. It isn't easy to see your beloved first daughter depart from your immediate influence and protection."

"You read me like a book, Wife. I missed her more than I thought I could while they were at Viamede," he admitted. "It is not that I wish to keep her here by my side. And she could not be in more trustworthy hands than Edward's. But to know that she will no longer be part of our household but mistress of her own — that I will no more be her guardian and teacher . . . ."

"You will always be her father, and as dear to her as she is to you," Rose said. "It is only the nature of your relationship that has changed, as it did when we married and I became her Mamma, as it did when she grew from a child to a young woman. Doesn't the Bible tell us that 'there is a time for everything, and a season for every activity under Heaven'? The season has altered for Elsie and for you. But the love you feel is changeless."

Horace put his free hand on Rose's arm and squeezed it affectionately.

"Just give me a little while to adjust to this new relationship," he sighed. "I suppose I shall feel the same when Trip and Rosie go out into the world."

"There are a good many years yet before we need worry about their leaving," Rose said, laughing lightly.

"And thankful I am of that," Horace replied, adding his laughter to hers, "for I am not ready for another change of season anytime soon."

The greeting at Ion was equally joyful but without the tinge of melancholy Horace felt. Mrs. Travilla was delighted to have her son home again, as she always was when he returned from a journey. And welcoming Elsie was one of the happiest moments the old lady had known for many years.

"My son and my daughter. I am so grateful to have you both home," she said, enfolding Elsie and Edward into her warm embrace. Never were words more true, for Mrs. Travilla felt all the love of a mother toward her new daughter-in-law. Elsie had been the answer to Mrs. Travilla's prayers — a good and true wife for Edward who loved him with all her heart and shared his deep and abiding Christian faith.

"It is so good to be back, Mrs. Travilla," Elsie said happily as she and Edward sat down for tea in his Mamma's charming sitting room.

Mrs. Travilla drew in her breath, and the expression on her face became oddly stern. "Now, Elsie," she began in a tone that was surprisingly strong. "While you are under this roof, you must obey my commands. I have only one, and it is that from this moment forward, you must address me by my proper name."

Elsie eyes widened. She could not imagine what she had done that was improper.

Elsie's Troubled Times

Then Mrs. Travilla's aged face softened into a beautiful smile, and she reached across the small tea table to take Elsie's hand.

"The proper way to address me, daughter of my house and my heart, is 'Mother'," she said, "unless you object to so familiar a name."

"Oh, no," Elsie exclaimed in relief and gratitude. "I have no objection at all, and I am honored to obey your command, Mother, as I will obey you in all matters."

"I don't think Mamma is likely to give you many orders, dearest," Edward said, casting a wry look at his mother.

"No, I shan't," Mrs. Travilla said, keeping her gaze on Elsie's lovely face. "You are mistress of Ion now, Elsie, and that is what I want."

"But I can never take your place," Elsie replied in earnest protest.

Mrs. Travilla leaned back in her chair again and laughed. "But you must, my dear. Believe me, that is exactly what I want and have for some years. The time has come for me to pass on the torch, and I could wish no better hands than yours in which to place this home and its people."

Elsie turned a doubtful look to her husband. She had no desire to usurp her mother-in-law's position, and she feared that Mrs. Travilla's words might reflect a sense of obligation more than a heartfelt desire to turn her authority over to an untried young woman.

"It's true," Edward said with assurance. "Long before I fell in love with you, dearest, my mamma was encouraging me to find a wife who would be mistress of this house. I tried to hire a housekeeper, but Mamma would have none of it. Only my wife would be fit to inherit her position."

Mrs. Travilla said, "Perhaps it was selfish of me, but I wanted a daughter, not hired help." She laughed a girlish little giggle. "I owe you an apology, Edward, for hounding you to marry. I should have realized that you would not wed until you found your true other half. I suppose that age made me anxious to see you happily settled. How glad I am that you followed your own heart and God's plan. With Elsie at your side, I can retire now in complete confidence and enjoy my declining years."

"I hope you will not retire quite yet, Mother," Elsie said. "I have so much to learn if I am to manage this household, and I hope you will be my teacher."

"That will be my great pleasure, darling," Mrs. Travilla replied. "I do love this old place, and I will be delighted to be of help to you in every way I can. But I also know that age must give youth its chance, and I have prayed to our Lord to give me the wisdom to know the difference between help and interference."

"I know that you will help Elsie as you have always helped me, Mamma," Edward said softly. "Never did a child have a more understanding parent than you. And never has an adult had a better friend and counselor."

"Hush now, Edward," Mrs. Travilla responded with mock seriousness. "This is a day for thanksgiving, and I will not allow you to make me cry like a sentimental old lady."

At just that moment, a servant entered bearing a large silver tray holding the tea things and several platters of sandwiches and small, iced cakes. He placed the heavy tray on the tea table and then excused himself. Mrs. Travilla, however, made no move toward the tray.

Instead, she bent toward Elsie and asked, "Will you serve the tea, Elsie dear? Let this be your first act as mistress of the house."

"I shall with pleasure, Mother," Elsie said, and a warm flush lit her face. She set about her new duty with grace and confidence.

Elsie's Troubled Times

Elsie's first months at Ion progressed busily. After their homecoming, she and Edward were honored at a number of parties almost as festive as the pre-wedding events, given that it was the holiday season. Everyone in the county, it seemed, wanted to entertain the newlyweds. But after several weeks, the social engagements slowed, and Elsie and Edward could settle into their new life as Mr. and Mrs. Travilla. In truth, they both enjoyed the comforts of Ion more than activities abroad and were content to remain by home and hearth.

Elsie eagerly undertook her new duties as mistress of the plantation. Mrs. Travilla was an excellent teacher, guiding Elsie through all the intricacies of running an extensive house and staff. Elsie, who had been largely sheltered by her father from most of the chores associated with household management, was amazed to discover how arduous and time-consuming the work was.

"I have more respect than ever for my dear Mamma," Elsie commented about her stepmother Rose on one March morning when she and Mrs. Travilla were reviewing the monthly accounts.

"Why is that, dear?" Mrs. Travilla asked a little abstractedly as she pondered a bill for kitchen supplies.

"Well, you know that she was younger than I when she left her family in Philadelphia, married Papa and came to The Oaks. Yet I never had any idea of how much work she must have been doing every day. Everything was always so perfect, and Mamma always so calm and self-assured."

"Your father was a great help to her," Mrs. Travilla said.

"Oh, I know he was, but still the house is her job, and she had me and then Trip and Rosie to care for as well," Elsie mused. Then she added in an urgent rush, "And what of you, dear Mother? You ran Ion alone for all those years when Edward was too young to assist you. A house and plantation and a child to rear—that was so brave of you."

Mrs. Travilla laid the kitchen bill aside and smiled at her daughter-in-law. "The work women do is usually appreciated at less than its true value. Children are naturally unaware of the daily responsibilities and worries of their parents, and a good parent does not begrudge her children's ignorance. But I do not think myself brave. I did what had to be done, and once I had accustomed myself to the work, I quite enjoyed myself. It must also be said that I am a fortunate mother. If Edward had been a difficult or resentful child, I am not sure that I could have managed this place on my own. In a way, he and I learned together, and he always wanted to help me. Many people thought I was selfish not to marry again and give Edward a new father. Had I found a man whom I could love as I did my dear husband, I would have married, but I do not believe that was God's plan for us."

"But the work must have been so hard for you," Elsie said questioningly.

"It was hard. There were many nights when I dragged myself to bed well past midnight and woke before dawn to tend to some task or other," Mrs. Travilla said. "But however long the days, whatever disputes I had to resolve — I always enjoyed the hard work and responsibility. God gave me physical strength and a good mind, and I felt that I was doing His will to maintain Ion as my husband had done. I think that you, too, enjoy work and responsibilities. I have seen how you manage your own businesses and how well you have taken on your duties here."

"Oh, I do enjoy it," Elsie said with enthusiasm. "I love to learn and then to put what I have learned into practice. That is how my Papa taught me. Still, I think that Edward was a fortunate child to have your example of pleasure in hard work. No burden ever seems to overwhelm him. I hope that I shall be able to teach my children as you taught him."

"You will be a good mother," Mrs. Travilla said with a gentle smile, then added, "in seven months or thereabouts, I should think."

Elsie's Troubled Times

Elsie's mouth dropped open at this unexpected remark. "How did you know?" she managed to say after several moments.

"I am very observant for an old lady with failing eyes," Mrs. Travilla replied.

Elsie laughed delightedly. "And I have not even told Edward, for I'm not absolutely sure myself. I plan to see Dr. Barton this very afternoon. But I should have known you would guess."

"I believe that the good doctor's diagnosis will be exactly what you hope for, dear Elsie. Excuse an old lady for giving advice, but if you are to have a baby, you should tell Edward immediately so that he may share every moment of this glorious experience with you. Fathers and mothers each have their role to play, but I have long felt that fathers should be involved with their children from the start."

The old lady's eyes suddenly became misty, and she said in a whisper, "I wish Horace had laid his eyes upon you on the day you were born. How much sadness and misunderstanding might never have occurred had he been there when you entered this world."

"I know," Elsie said, recalling her lonely childhood. "But this will be different, Mother. I will have Edward at my side, and you, and Papa and Mamma."

Mrs. Travilla laughed, "If it is true, then I will be a grandmother at last. And Horace Dinsmore will be a grandpa! Think of that. Mischievous little Horace, who used to play soldier in my flower beds and once put a frog in Edward's nanny's nightstand — a grandfather!"

Elsie covered her mother-in-law's hand with her own. "It is an amazing thing. But I think we should follow the advice Aunt Chloe so often gives and not count our chickens before they hatch. Dr. Barton is coming at three, and then we shall know for certain."

"You are right, my dear," Mrs. Travilla said, her voice sober but her soft eyes sparkling. "I'll say nothing until we hear the doctor's verdict. But just in case, I believe I shall add some extra yarn to my order this month. I may have a great deal of knitting to do."

CHAPTER

A Time To Be Born

"For you created my inmost being; you knit me together in my mother's womb."

PSALM 139:13

*T*hat very day, Dr. Barton confirmed Mrs. Travilla's guess. Elsie and Edward Travilla were to become parents. Edward was overjoyed when Elsie told him the news. But he would not allow the doctor to depart Ion until he had been questioned about everything that must be done to assure Elsie's good health and the baby's.

"Don't you dare pamper and indulge your wife," the doctor finally said in amused impatience. "Elsie is strong. She can attend to all her duties for some time yet, so don't go coddling her like one of your hothouse flowers. She may feel a little ill in the mornings, but that will pass soon. Just see that she eats well and gets her rest. And whatever questions you two have, ask your mother first, Edward. If there should be any problem—which I don't anticipate—you know that I will come day or night. You first-time fathers are all alike. Just relax, man, and let nature take its course. God is giving you both a wonderful gift. My best guess is that sometime near the end of September, you will be the father of a robust baby boy or girl."

Reassured, Edward finally allowed Dr. Barton to continue on his rounds. The doctor bade his good-byes to Elsie and Mrs. Travilla, and then Edward accompanied him to the driveway.

As Dr. Barton was about to climb into his buggy, he stopped and spoke seriously to Edward. "Believe me, Elsie is fine. I can see no reason why she and your child should not come through this in excellent condition. But she may worry, given her own mother's early death after childbirth. You can assure her that her circumstances are completely different. Her mother was very young, and she had been severely weakened by grief and worry. That is not the case with Elsie. Just exercise reasonable caution and good sense, and all should go well."

"I will," Edward said earnestly. "Forgive me for being overly concerned, but this announcement has taken me by surprise."

"I understand. However, there is another matter," Dr. Barton said, lowering his voice. "I want you to keep a careful eye on your mother. She is not as young as she once was, nor as strong as she thinks. And as you know, she has not been well this past year. I haven't found anything amiss other than the inevitable infirmities of age, but I know that she is sometimes inclined to push herself beyond the limits of her strength. Don't let her tax herself or over-exert."

Edward's handsome face had turned pale at the doctor's words.

"Are you saying—" he began, but Dr. Barton cut him off.

"I am saying only that your mother is past seventy, and you must watch out for her. Common sense, my boy. Now you go back inside and celebrate with Elsie and Mrs. Travilla. I have other people to see today."

Edward took the doctor at his word. He was watchful of both his wife and his mother, but not excessive in his precautions.

Elsie's Papa, on the other hand, would have gladly wrapped his daughter in cotton wool and had her waited upon hand and foot. When informed of Elsie and Edward's good news, Horace was overwhelmed by old memories of Elsie's mother and guilt at his abandonment of his first wife and child when they most needed him. To compensate for that long-ago failure, he became insistent that Elsie move back to her old suite at The Oaks for the duration of her pregnancy. His fear for Elsie's life was so great at first that he could not even find pleasure in the advent of his first grandchild. It took much prayer and self-examination, many long talks with Rose and one severe lecture from Dr. Barton to settle Horace's mind and calm his worries. But once he realized that his fears were unfounded (and, he was forced to admit, more selfish than selfless), he put them away, placed his full faith in God's tender mercy, and determined to make the impending event as easy for Elsie and Edward as he could.

The immediate result was that Elsie spent many pleasant days in her father's house. Rose was a source of excellent advice, when asked, and constant support to Elsie. Young Trip, still under thirteen, was too reserved to make a show of his feelings, but inwardly he was thrilled at the prospect of his first niece or nephew. And little Rosie bubbled with excitement every time she talked of the new "babbie" in the family. Horace, who could not entirely rid himself of his anxiousness for Elsie's well-being, was nevertheless the considerate father to her, offering whatever she required for her comfort but insisting on nothing.

At Ion the sense of anticipation grew almost palpable as the summer died away and the final days of September approached. Aunt Chloe and Old Joe oversaw the preparations for the nursery, and Chloe instructed her granddaughter, Dinah — selected by Elsie to be the baby's nursemaid — in every aspect of the care of infants. Mrs. Travilla worked out her excitement on endless pairs of knitted boots and stockings and baby jackets and embroidered items for the baby's layette.

As for Elsie, the joy in her heart radiated in her face. As her confinement approached, she and Edward had a number of deep discussions about their parenthood. It was natural that they spent hours deciding on names for both a boy and a girl and that they discussed their child's future — issues such as discipline and education. But their most intense talks concerned their obligations to bring up the baby in the faith that was the foundation of their life together. They prayed for His blessings and His guidance to lead their child in the ways of the Lord, to love always and to teach love by their words and deeds. They prayed for patience and wisdom and courage.

Elsie's Troubled Times

On the last day of September, Elsie woke just after dawn with the pains that signaled the coming of her child. She roused Edward with the words, "It is time."

Edward immediately summoned Chloe, and Chloe summoned Joe, and Joe ran to find the head groomsman and sent him for Dr. Barton. And Dinah arrived and hurried Edward out of the bedroom.

"It's going be some time before that baby comes, Mr. Edward," Dinah said firmly, "and you might as well dress now and get yourself a good meal and go on about your business. My Grandpa is going to sit outside that door all day and he'll come find you the minute something happens."

Edward, feeling a little dazed but grateful for Dinah's efficiency, asked, "Is there nothing I can do?"

"Not here you can't," she replied smartly. "There's no reason to wake your mother neither. Grandma Chloe and I will take good care of Miss Elsie. But you might want to send word over to the folks at The Oaks. I know that Mister Horace has been sitting on pins and needles ever since he first heard this day was coming."

"Can I see my wife?"

Dinah laughed heartily. "Course you can, Mr. Edward, just as soon as you get some breakfast." Then she softened her tone and smiled at him. "It's best to let my Grandma get Miss Elsie settled down right now, sir. First babies mostly take their own good time arriving, so let us make your wife comfortable. Wait about an hour. Then you come in to see her and squeeze her hand and tell her how proud you are of her. That's the best kind of help you can be."

Edward smiled back at the young woman. "Thank you, Dinah," he said. "This is a new experience for me, and I'm grateful for your assistance. I will do as you instruct."

"And don't you worry, sir," Dinah said as Edward hurried down the hall to his dressing room. "Miss Elsie's going to do just fine."

A Time To Be Born

Elsie's labor was not so long as might have been expected, and in the mid-afternoon, Chloe came out of the bedroom and grabbed her husband's arm.

Joe jumped to his feet.

"Well," he demanded, "what is it?"

"A baby, of course," Chloe said. "As healthy as can be, and Miss Elsie come through it just as fit as a fiddle. They're both gonna be just fine."

"But what is it—boy or girl?"

"That's for Mr. Edward to hear first. Now you go on down and tell him Dr. Barton says to come on up here. I'm thinking he's waiting with Mrs. Travilla and Elsie's Papa and Mamma in the sitting room. Tell them the doctor says for Mr. Edward to come right now and the rest in about half an hour. Elsie's tired out, but she wants to see them all before she rests."

"Then you gonna tell me whether we got a boy or a girl? I've been sittin' here a long time to have to wait much longer for that news."

"Do what the doctor says, then come back yourself, and I'll tell you."

So Joe hurried off, and Chloe took his place in the chair by the bedroom door. She sat very still for perhaps a minute; then almost beyond her notice, her hand began to shake and large tears rolled down her cheeks.

"Thank You, dear Lord, for bringing my baby and her baby through this safe and sound," she prayed in a gruff whisper. "You know how much Elsie means to me, and I'm mighty thankful You've seen to it she's going to be with us for a long time. And thank You for giving her a strong and beautiful baby. Bless her, Heavenly Father, and Mr. Edward and their infant. And Dr. Barton, too, 'cause he's a fine doctor and a good man. Amen."

Elsie's Troubled Times

Chloe had returned to her duties, and Dr. Barton was just stepping out of the bedroom when Edward ran toward him. The physician's broad grin conveyed the message Edward was desperate for.

"She's well?" he asked.

"Tired, of course, but she came through with her colors flying, and the baby as well," Dr. Barton replied. "She should stay in bed for a few days, but then let her get up as soon as she feels like it. I don't expect any complications. I've given instructions to Aunt Chloe, and I will come back tomorrow to make sure all is well."

Edward put his hand on the doorknob but hesitated. "You are certain they are both alright?" he asked.

"Certain as rain," the doctor laughed. "But see for yourself, man. She's waiting for you. I'll go downstairs and speak to your mother and Rose and Horace, if that meets your approval. May I send them to see Elsie in a half hour? I doubt that Horace will wait much longer."

"Please do," Edward said. "And I believe that Lavinia has prepared a very special meal for you, if you have time to stay."

"I accept and gladly," the doctor replied, putting a firm hand on Edward's arm. "Now open that door and go to your wife and child."

Edward entered the room as quietly as he could. Elsie was sitting up in their bed, a great pile of snowy pillows supporting her and highlighting the rich brown curls that tumbled about her shoulders. Aunt Chloe was just putting a small bundle of blanket into Elsie's arms, and Dinah was smoothing down the fresh bedcovers.

"Come on in, Mr. Edward," Chloe said with a warm smile. "Miss Elsie has someone for you to meet."

A Time To Be Born

As Edward approached the bed, the two servant women slipped past him and out the door, closing it behind them.

Elsie looked up at her husband, and though Edward could see the fatigue in her pale face, her eyes sparkled.

"I cannot stop staring at her, Edward," Elsie said. "Your daughter is perfect, my beloved."

Edward bent down and looked into the bundle where a tiny face could be seen.

With the gentlest motion, Edward touched the baby's forehead and pushed the blanket back to reveal a crown of downy hair as black as his own.

"This is your father, little one," Elsie said softly. "He wants to hold you."

Carefully, Edward sat on the edge of the bed and took his baby into his arms. The little face turned toward him, and the baby made a series of purrs and squeaks.

"Can she see me?" he asked.

"I don't think so. Not as I see you. Not yet," Elsie answered. "But she can feel your touch and the comfort of your embrace."

"She is so very small," Edward said in a tone of amazement.

"In fact, Dr. Barton says that she is a little larger than average," Elsie commented proudly, "and that is to her advantage. Babies lose some of their weight in the early days, you know."

"I didn't know," Edward replied. Then he added, "She is very red, isn't she?"

Elsie laughed. "You would be red, too, if you were less than an hour old. But she really is perfect, Edward. I have counted all her fingers and all her toes, and there are just the right number."

As if in response to this remark, five tiny fingers emerged from the blanket and curled around Edward's index finger. Their soft touch was like a shock to him, and he instinctively pressed his lips to the baby's forehead. Then he turned to his wife and kissed her with equal gentleness on her cheek.

Elsie's Troubled Times

"And you, my love, how do you feel?"

"Tired, dearest, but otherwise I am glorious. God has been so good to us this day, Edward. Can there be anything more wonderful than bringing a new life into this world?"

Edward looked back at his squirming, cooing daughter.

"So new and pure and innocent," he said, his voice made hoarse by the overpowering emotion he felt. "I love you, little Elsie, and your Mamma loves you, and God loves you. May He bless you for all the days of your life."

"And may He welcome you into His house and hold you in His loving arms now and forever," Elsie whispered to her first-born.

⟡

"A granddaughter!" Mrs. Travilla exclaimed when Dr. Barton made his announcement to the anxious little group in the sitting room.

"And another Elsie," Dr. Barton went on, greatly enjoying his role as the bearer of good tidings. "Elsie tells me that her name is to be Elsie for her own mother and"—he looked into Mrs. Travilla's shining face—"Eugenia for her father's mother."

Tears sprang to the old lady's eyes. "Named for me?" she managed to say. "I don't believe I have ever felt so honored."

Rose came to sit close beside her friend, handing Mrs. Travilla a lace handkerchief from her sleeve. Horace crossed the room to Dr. Barton, extending his hand.

"You have seen Elsie through illness and pain," Horace said, "and now through this most joyful event, my good friend. How can I ever thank you adequately for the care you have given to my daughter and her baby?"

"Ah," began Dr. Barton, a little embarrassed now by the attention. "No thanks are necessary, Horace. In my work, days like today, when I can help a healthy new life begin, are my greatest reward. But remember, it is your Elsie who has done the hardest work."

"And she's really well?" Horace said, a cloud of uncertainty momentarily crossing his face.

"She's fine!" the doctor exclaimed, slapping his friend's shoulder. "She'll be up in a matter of days, and back to her old self nearly as soon."

"But shouldn't she rest for several weeks at least?" Horace asked.

"No, no, Horace. She's a new mother, not an invalid. I appeal to you, Mrs. Dinsmore," Dr. Barton said, turning to Rose. "Don't let this proud new grandpa treat his daughter like a china doll."

Rose smiled and said, "I will do my best, sir, but you know she is the apple of his eye."

"Seriously, Horace," the doctor continued, "I will keep a careful watch over Elsie and the child. And Aunt Chloe and Dinah will attend to their every need. You have no call to worry."

He then glanced at his pocket watch and said, "Now then, Edward tells me that Lavinia has prepared something special, and as I have not dined since breakfast, I will avail myself of your hospitality, Mrs. Travilla."

"Of course, Dr. Barton," Mrs. Travilla answered gaily as Rose helped her to rise from the couch. "You have more than earned your supper today."

"While I retire to the dining room and your cook's excellent cuisine," the doctor said, "I believe it is time for all of you to go upstairs. I told Edward that I would send you up in half an hour. Go on now. The moment has come for the new Miss Elsie Eugenia Travilla to meet her grandparents."

CHAPTER

A Time To Mourn

*"Even though I walk through the
valley of the shadow of death,
I will fear no evil, for you
are with me; your rod
and your staff, they
comfort me."*

PSALM 23:4

*I*t is impossible to describe the happiness that the new arrival brought. It had been many years since there was a child at Ion, and the presence of the infant girl seemed to lift the spirits and gladden the hearts of every member of the household.

"I believe she will have your hazel eyes," said Edward one morning when the baby was nearly six weeks old. He was holding his daughter while Elsie busied herself changing the sheets in the delicate oaken cradle that still had its place in their bedroom.

"And your dark hair," Elsie replied.

"But with your ringlets, I think," said the proud papa. "See how it already begins to curl about my finger? Elsie, does it seem to you that she has a particularly good disposition? There, see how she smiles at me."

Elsie laid down the little blanket she was folding and came to stand beside her husband's chair. She, too, gazed on the remarkably pretty little face, and said slowly, "Well, perhaps she cries a little less than most. She does eat well and has not been at all colicky or cranky. Dinah has commented on her happy temperament, and Aunt Chloe says she has the disposition of an angel, but Aunt Chloe is biased."

"And we are not?" Edward laughed.

"Of course we are, but I try to be honest with myself. I do fear, dearest, that I will be inclined to spoil her. Without mother or father, my own childhood was so lonely. But I do not want to err in the opposite direction and smother my own child with indulgences."

"Our little Miss is far too young to be spoiled just yet," Edward said as he rocked his gurgling child, "but I share your concern. In the pleasure of having her with us, I have to remind myself that children are not the possessions of their parents, but only lent to us that we may bring them up in the ways of our Heavenly Father. I don't want to be one of those parents who see only themselves and their ambitions in their children. That always seems to lead to over-indulgence on the one hand or too severe discipline on the other."

"Rose said something like that when she was here yesterday," Elsie remarked. "Mamma said that it is tempting for many mothers and fathers to see their children as little versions of themselves and forget that all children are the unique creations of God."

"Was she speaking of her own children?" Edward asked in surprise. "I think she is doing an excellent job with Trip and Rosie."

"As a matter of fact, we were talking of Arthur Dinsmore and how he has improved himself so greatly in the last few years, since his accident."

"I must admit that I never thought that boy could turn himself around. Never did I know so spoiled and selfish a lad as he. But he has made real changes for the better."

"Mamma was making the point that he might have been a happier child and young man if Grandpa and Mrs. Dinsmore had treated him differently. Mrs. Dinsmore spoiled him dreadfully because he was her first son and she saw herself in him. And Grandpa was always disappointed in him because he was not just like my Papa. In a way, Arthur was never allowed to be the person God intended him to be. There was always goodness in him, though it lay buried beneath his anger and cynicism."

"And he has hidden courage, too. I shall always be grateful for the way Arthur stood up to Tom Jackson and warned us of the danger that scoundrel posed, though his own life was put in jeopardy."

Elsie laid a finger against her child's soft cheek and was rewarded with a pink smile. "I want our little one to become the person God intends her to be."

"Then you must be prepared to discipline her at times," Edward said teasingly. "When she pours jam on the tablecloth or causes mischief, you must be stern with her."

"And love her all the while," Elsie replied, dropping a gentle kiss on her child's face then turning back to her chores.

Edward, who also had all manner of pressing business to attend to, nevertheless gave himself several precious minutes more with his daughter.

"So you think her good disposition and charming smiles may simply be the result of not having colic?" he asked Elsie, returning to the original topic of their conversation.

"I said no such thing!" Elsie exclaimed with a laugh. "I meant only that we should not let our parental pride and love lead us to see perfection rather than the wonderful human being who has been placed in our care."

"And I accept the truth of what you say, but I cannot think it all pride that I see an especially beautiful child here in my arms," Edward said. "If my eyes do not deceive me, little Missy of mine," he cooed to the infant, "you have inherited all of your mother's beauty."

As he lowered his face close to the wiggling bundle, a small hand suddenly darted up and grabbed his nose.

Elsie, who had observed this little scene, laughed again. "I believe that she has inherited your sense of humor, dear husband. Just look at how your nose makes her smile."

Little Missy, as everyone in the family now called her, grew straight and strong and remained cheerful in temperament. In loving their child, Elsie and Edward felt closer to one another than they had dreamed possible. But their life at Ion was not without its shadow.

Elsie's Troubled Times

When the baby was six months old, her grandmother suffered a sudden attack, and Dr. Barton's prognosis was not good.

"It's her heart," he told Edward and Elsie on the evening Mrs. Travilla became ill. "There is nothing I can do to heal the damage. However, I believe she will recover from this incident, and I know she will receive the best care possible. She will regain some of her strength, but she must be watched carefully. Any exertion or anxiety can bring on a repeat, and I fear she has not the strength to survive another attack."

"Then she is dying," Edward said. His face had turned ashen and showed lines of strain that Elsie had never seen before.

"She is living near the end of her existence on this earth," Dr. Barton replied gently, "but none of us can predict the time of her going. That is God's decision. It would be wrong to treat your mother as if she were at death's door, my friend. Her heart is very weak, and you should protect her from exertion and worry. But do not make the mistake of babying her now. Talk with her as you always have. Your mother is an extraordinary woman, Edward, and though her body is failing, her mind is as sharp as ever and her spirit as strong."

Edward walked with halting steps to the sofa where Elsie sat, and he slumped down beside her. With a short gasp that sounded like a sob, he moaned, "I cannot imagine my life without her."

In a tone sharper than he intended, Dr. Barton said, "She has not gone yet and may be with us, God willing, for some time. But you will kill her, Edward, if you steal her dignity and treat her as someone to be cosseted and coddled. I've seen it happen too many times in my practice. You must focus on her happiness and not your grief. The time for grieving will come, but not now, man. Remember your faith. Your mother understands how ill she is, but she is facing this final journey with hope and anticipation of her welcome from our God and Savior in Heaven. Do not deprive her of her joy by burdening her with your sorrow."

Edward raised his head, and Elsie could see that some of his natural color had returned. She took his hand and felt only the slightest of tremors.

"Is she suffering pain?" Edward asked the doctor.

"No, just great weakness."

"Then tell us what we are to do," Edward said, his voice now calm and steady.

"I will give you full instructions. Aunt Chloe has expressed her wish to be Mrs. Travilla's nurse, and I think that is an excellent idea, if you can spare your maid, Elsie."

"Of course," Elsie replied instantly. "Chloe is the best of nursemaids, and a good companion as well. She and Mother have been through much together over the years and are close friends. But what are we to do—Edward and I?"

"What you have always done. Love your mother, protect her, cherish your time with her, and learn from her. Allow her the company of her granddaughter. I believe that your child may be the best of all tonics. The very young have a way of accepting the infirmities of the old that their parents do not. Perhaps it is because they do not yet understand death that they do not feel fear. At any rate, Mrs. Travilla adores her namesake, so give her time with the child."

The doctor looked down on the anguished couple who were so dear to him. "I know that this is a terrible shock and a great sadness to you both, but as you tend to your mother, you must also tend to yourselves. Guard your own health so that you can be strong for Mrs. Travilla. Adjust your duties as needed, but don't ignore your work and the rest of your family. This plantation has been your mother's life, Edward. She saved it and built it up for you and your children. Do not let your sorrow distract you from the work that must be done to preserve her legacy."

Elsie's Troubled Times

Edward stood and crossed the room to where the doctor stood. He had recovered his firm step now.

"How do I speak to my mother of this?" he asked.

"Let her be your guide, dear friend. I feel certain she will want to talk much of her faith and her hope and perhaps even of her fears," Dr. Barton said. Then he smiled and continued, "Your mother is one of the wisest and most realistic women I have ever known. There will be practical issues she wishes to discuss. I know that you will not dissuade her or try to make light of serious matters. Just remember that she is preparing for the greatest journey that any person of faith will take. When the time comes, she will be going home, Edward, to her Heavenly Father and Savior. She will not be lost to you in the way that counts, and you will see her again. Make the most of the days left to you both in this world, and look forward to the time when you will be together again in the next."

"It is strange that at my age I have never really faced death in this way," Edward was saying to Elsie later that night as they sat together in bed. She was holding him in her arms as he had so often held her. She wanted so much to be his strength now.

"I was so young when my father died that I barely remember him. Oh, I knew he was gone, and I missed him. But I did not have a lifetime of his care and love and wisdom as I have had from Mamma. She has always been my rock."

"You have been blessed by God to have her," Elsie said.

"I have been," he agreed, "and Dr. Barton was right. She is not gone, and I cannot presume to know our Father's plan for her or anyone. I must make the most of all the time we have left together."

"I, too," Elsie whispered, laying her head on her husband's shoulder.

A Time To Mourn

As they sat in this silent embrace, a soft gurgle followed by a gentle sigh came to their ears from the cradle near the bed.

"God's plan is truly wondrous," Edward said. "He gave us this new life in time for Mamma to share in it. The one does not replace the other, but through our little Elsie Eugenia, my Mamma's memory will continue on to new generations. That is a comforting thought in this sad time."

A verse from the Book of Lamentations came suddenly to Elsie's mind, and she quoted, "'Though He brings grief, He will show compassion, so great is His unfailing love.'"

As Dr. Barton had predicted, Mrs. Travilla was never to regain her full strength after her heart attack. Winter had just ended when she fell ill, but spring was rapidly turning to summer before she could leave her bed again. The mildest of activities wearied her now, and she found it difficult to converse with her family or old friends for more than a few minutes at a time. The shortest walks made her breathless, and climbing stairs was impossible, so Elsie and Edward converted the downstairs sitting room—always Mrs. Travilla's favorite retreat—into a comfortable bedroom with an extra bed for Chloe, who tended her patient night and day.

But still the gentle old lady loved life and betrayed not a hint of bitterness at her failing condition. Edward ordered a wheelchair from the city so that he could take his mother on strolls through the gardens and the greenhouses. Mrs. Travilla was too weak and her sight too poor for her favorite pastimes of sewing and knitting, but the garden still gave her immense pleasure, especially in its showy summer displays. In the evenings, Edward or Elsie read to her and held their devotions with her.

Elsie's Troubled Times

She now dined in her room, and Edward and Elsie sometimes joined her there, taking their meals on trays. Mrs. Travilla loved hearing of the events of the day—the preparation of a new field for a crop of late corn, the birth of a new baby in the quarters, the overseer's plans to renovate one of the outbuildings. All that happened at Ion interested her, and she was not hesitant to make suggestions when she thought her ideas of merit.

Edward and Elsie spent as much time as they could with her, sometimes talking but just as often sitting in companionable silence. Horace and Rose came frequently to Ion, and sometimes brought Trip and Rosie, who delighted in playing with their new niece. Horace Dinsmore, Sr., made several calls, for he had always regarded Mrs. Travilla as a valued friend and neighbor, and the thought of losing her caused him deep but unexpressed sorrow. The minister came weekly, and his visits always cheered Mrs. Travilla. And Dr. Barton dropped in much more often than his professional duties required. (He once brought a distinguished specialist who was visiting from the North. The physician examined Mrs. Travilla, yet, alas, he could only confirm Dr. Barton's diagnosis.)

Every day, without fail, little Missy was taken to her grandmother's room, and these visits were as welcome as manna from Heaven. One late summer afternoon, Elsie was sitting and sewing while her mother-in-law rested and Missy played with some wooden toys on the rug. Elsie thought Mrs. Travilla had drifted off to sleep, so she focused on her work while keeping her mind's eye on her child. Suddenly she was startled by a weak but excited little exclamation: "Look at the child, Elsie!"

Elsie looked first at the bed where her Mother lay, but Mrs. Travilla was not in distress. A grin actually played upon her pale, thin face, and with a shaky finger, she pointed to the floor.

Elsie turned her gaze upon Missy and beheld her child's first, wobbly steps. Missy managed five or six before collapsing to the floor in a burst of giggles.

Elsie started to reach for her baby, but Mrs. Travilla said, "Let her try again, dear Daughter. You must always protect your children from harm without impeding their independence."

Elsie sat back in her chair and watched in wonderment. Missy quickly crawled to her grandmother's bed, and using the bedpost, she pulled herself upright. She steadied herself, clinging to the post. Then with a look of intense concentration, the little figure stepped forward again, her tiny legs carrying her in a comic path from the bed to her mother. Elsie swept Missy into a joyful embrace, and Mrs. Travilla laughed softly. "Thank you, Father, for allowing me this moment," she said.

Little Missy practiced her new skill all that afternoon, and by the time Edward returned to the house, his daughter was able to walk a short but nearly straight path into his arms.

Autumn in the South tends to be muted compared to the rest of the country, a pastel version of the brilliant red, orange, and gold landscapes of New England and the northern states. But some years, when the weather has been just right and the rains generous, every maple and oak and poplar is painted with the brightest hues. This autumn season at Ion, arriving several weeks after the family celebrated Missy's first birthday, was such a phenomenon—a glorious blaze of hot colors set against the deep blue skies of clear, warm days.

"It is as if our Heavenly Father has painted the fields and forests to give Mamma's failing eyes a sight she cannot mistake," Edward said to Elsie as they prepared to go to his mother's room for supper.

"She sat in her wheelchair on the porch for two hours this afternoon," Elsie reported. "She was as alert as I have seen her in months, and her voice was stronger. She spoke of Ion and your father and your boyhood. She told me the details of an event that my Papa mentioned to me many years ago — when you and he and several other boys were squirrel hunting and he was nearly shot."

Edward smiled at the memory. "Thinking back, I believe that bullet missed him more widely than we believed. But never was a group of boys more frightened."

"Mother said that she punished you even though it was not your rifle that fired the shot."

"She did, indeed. I was deprived of my gun for several weeks, and she forbade me to hunt for the rest of that season. She said that at Ion, I was responsible for the thoughtless and dangerous actions of my friends. It was a good lesson. I probably felt guiltier than the careless boy who pulled the trigger. If Horace had been wounded or killed, my remorse and grief would have been no less than the accidental assassin's."

"So God saved my Papa and taught you all a valuable lesson."

"He did, and my Mamma made certain that the lesson was learned."

"Was she always strict with you?"

"Not at all. She could indulge me shamelessly when the occasion suited, but that was not often. I would say she had a gift for striking the proper balance between discipline and indulgence. And she never disciplined without clearly explaining the reasons for her action. I was not overly naughty," he added with a laugh, "but I had many lessons to learn, and Mamma saw that I did."

"Do you think we should tell her our news tonight?" Elsie asked, moving to the subject that was uppermost in her mind.

"Now that Dr. Barton has confirmed it, I want to share it with Mamma immediately. There is little more we can do for her now than we are doing. This will be a gift for her," Edward replied. He moved to his wife and encircled her waist with his arms.

"It was just a week or so ago that Mamma mentioned how Missy needed a playmate. Do you think she already suspects?" he asked.

"She knew about Missy almost as soon as I did," Elsie said. "I would not be surprised if she is ahead of us this time as well."

She reached up and brushed a lock of hair back from his forehead. "Do you wish for a boy this time, my love?"

"That seems the expected wish for a father," he answered, "but in truth, I care less whether it is a boy or a girl than that it is healthy and that you are fine. Besides, Missy already has us well trained to be the parents of girls," he joked.

Elsie's lovely face softened. "I hope Mother will be with us to love this baby as she loves Missy."

"It is in God's hands, dearest," Edward said. "Whatever happens, it is all in His good time."

Autumn's brilliant fire died out quickly and was followed by an unusually early and sustained period of cold. Heavy frosts in November and snows in December were followed by ice storms in January. Day after day of gray skies and dreary dampness made it feel as if the whole world had gone into mourning. As winter's hand tightened its grip on the land, Mrs. Travilla moved closer to her final days.

When she could muster the strength, she met with Elsie and Edward. Her lawyer came to Ion from the city, and Mrs. Travilla also held private talks with her son and with her minister. Every day, little Missy was brought to her bedside briefly, and for those moments the old woman brightened as if sunlight had suddenly flooded her face. But toward the end of January, she suffered another attack, and though she lived through it, Dr. Barton could offer no hope.

"Her heart can no longer sustain her," he told Edward. "It is but a matter of hours, perhaps a day, before it fails entirely. You must prepare yourself, my friend."

"May I see her?"

"She has asked for you. Do not worry about tiring her. She needs you at her side."

With those words, the doctor left, burdened by a sense of loss greater than he had felt in a very long time.

When Edward entered his mother's room, he was stunned by the change in her. So pale was her face upon the pillow that she seemed hardly to exist at all. He pulled a chair close by the bed, sat down, and took her hand in both of his. It was surprisingly warm and dry, yet seemed to have no more weight than a sparrow's wing.

"Mamma," he said in a whisper. "I am here with you."

Her eyelids fluttered open, and a small, sweet smile came to her lips.

"My son," she said, her voice as thin as the breezes of summer. "I know you will miss me, but you must not fear for me. I have come to the end of this road, and now I travel a new and glorious path. Mourn me as you must, dear boy, but know in your heart that I am happy. I am going home. In that home, we will be together again some day."

"Jesus is waiting for you, Mamma," he said, his voice catching on every word, "and I am glad for that. He has given us many good years together. I am glad you feel no fear."

"One only fears the unknown," she said, "yet I know that He awaits me. God has instructed us all, 'Fear not, for I have redeemed you . . . .'"

Her voice trailed away, and Edward took up the Holy words: "'I have summoned you by name; you are mine. When you pass through the waters, I will be with you; and when you pass through the rivers, they will not sweep over you. When you walk through the fire, you will not be burned . . . . Do not be afraid for I am with you . . . .'"

He fell silent, leaning close until he could hear the soft, labored in and out of his mother's slow breathing. He did not feel, as he had so often over the past six months, the frustrating impulse to do something in order to make her well, to somehow convey his strength to her. Edward accepted that the end was near, and he discovered that he was, despite his deep sadness, truly happy for her.

He held her weightless hand and looked upon her sleeping face for a very long time, it seemed, until she awoke and spoke once more.

"Bring Elsie and the others, my son. I must say my farewells."

Edward did as he was directed, and soon they were all gathered in the room — Elsie, Horace and Rose. The minister had arrived, and he joined them as well. Chloe sat by the fire, weeping without sound, and Lavinia, who had cooked and kept house for Mrs. Travilla for some thirty years, stood quietly at the side of Chloe's chair, a small Bible gripped tightly in her hands. Edward had taken his seat beside his mother and held her hand.

Everyone was taken by surprise when Mrs. Travilla opened her eyes and asked first for Lavinia. The servant came quickly to her side.

"I have given instructions to Edward that from this day forward, Lavinia, you are a free woman," the old woman said in the clearest of tones. "You served me with loyalty and kindness for many years, and my death shall be a new life for you. Edward will explain it all, but know this, Lavinia, that I have loved you and wronged you. Please forgive me."

"Oh, Miss Eugenia," Lavinia cried. "I do forgive, and I will miss you, ma'am, more than I can say."

"Perhaps others may follow my example," Mrs. Travilla said softly. Then with great effort she turned her head to the others. "Horace, Rose, farewell, my dear friends, until we meet again before the throne. Elsie, come close. God bless you, child, for you have brought me all the joy and comfort of a true daughter. Watch over our Missy and the new baby and tell them someday how much I loved them."

At that her eyes drifted closed again, and her head sank back into the pillow. From across the room came the gentle voice of the minister as he recited the Twenty-third Psalm. When he had finished, Mrs. Travilla whispered so softly that only Edward could make out her words. Squeezing his hand in a last burst of strength, she said, "He calls me now. I love you, Edward. God loves you. God loves you all."

And she was gone.

⌒

The skies cleared, and the sun smiled on the countryside on the day they buried Mrs. Travilla beside her husband in the family cemetery. Tears were shed, and the many friends and family members who gathered at the graveside were appropriately reverent. Yet the mood was not somber; a spirit of hope and thankfulness pervaded the simple service.

"We have come to say good-bye to a woman who touched us all with her good heart and godly ways," the minister said. "She was wife, mother, grandmother, mistress of this estate, and friend. She loved God absolutely and put her complete trust in Him. She strove to serve Him and to follow His commandments every day and in every way. She never expected more of others than she demanded of herself. She always gave more than she took. Her passing grieves us all. But to those she has left behind I say, take your comfort in the knowledge that this good woman, redeemed by the sacrifice of our Lord and Savior, has crossed the river Jordan. Be joyful, friends. God has called her home, and she now dwells in His house."

Then, for the second time in as many days, he offered the Twenty-third Psalm for Mrs. Travilla.

CHAPTER

Recovery

"Blessed are those who mourn, for they will be comforted."

Matthew 5:4

Recovery

$\mathcal{E}$dward, as a Christian, believed with all his heart that his mother was with God, and he rejoiced for her. Still, it was hard for him to lose the one whose constancy had been his support for almost forty years. He would enter her sitting room or the parlor and half expect to see her there. Everything in the house reminded him of her, and there was no place he could go without remembering her. One day he found a piece of partly completed embroidery tucked under the cushion of a couch, and the sight of the work of his mother's hands brought forth a rush of emotion so intense that he could not control it. Hot tears fell from his eyes for some time, and sobs shook him to the very core of his being. In this storm, he at last found release.

He remembered something she had told him many years before. He had been about twelve, and he had asked her how she felt when his father died. "At first I thought my heart would break," she'd replied, "but then I looked into your face, and I understood that in you, a part of your father would always be with me. If I let my grief overwhelm me, I would dishonor his memory and deny you the fullness of my affection. You see, my son, grief for those who are gone must never diminish our love for those who remain."

By her own life, his mother had shown him how to endure terrible loss, and he determined to follow her lesson. He had too much love in his heart—for Elsie, for Missy, for the child who was coming—to let himself become obsessed with his grief.

Wiping away the remnants of his tears, he became aware that he was smiling.

"You are still teaching me, Mamma," he said aloud to the empty room. "And I am still learning. Dear Lord," he prayed, "thank You for giving me the wisest and most loving of parents. Help me now to find the strength to be guided by her example."

God answered his prayer, and from that moment on, Edward was troubled no more by the shadows of his loss.

Elsie, who was extremely sensitive to her husband's moods, understood the depths of his private grief and knew better than to afflict him with the platitudes and clichés that people usually say to the grieving. She comforted where she could, and she trusted Edward to come to terms with his sorrow in his own time. But she also felt the loss of her mother-in-law keenly.

"I wish Mother had lived to see her new grandchild," she said to her husband. It was the evening of the day Edward had experienced his emotional revelation, and he had just joined her in the library, to await the supper bell.

"Don't feel regret, dearest. Mamma lived to see us become parents and to know our Missy. If we look for things to regret, we will always find them. I want to remember how happy Mamma was to the last. Do you recall the day when Missy took her first step?" he asked.

Elsie, who had been concentrating on a shirt sleeve she was mending, heard a new quality in his voice. She looked up at him and saw, for this first time since the beginning of Mrs. Travilla's illness, that his face was unclouded by sorrow. The lines of pain and stress had vanished. There was laughter in his eyes, and he looked as he did when he was thirty.

Without thinking, she said, "I do believe, Husband, that you have turned back the hands of time today. You seem to have lost ten or more years since breakfast!"

"That is an odd reply to my question," he laughed. "It is a compliment, I think."

"Oh, yes, Edward, though poorly stated," she replied. She rose from her seat and came to stand close by his chair. "I meant only that the worry and sorrow of this last year seem to have fled from you. You know I've always believed you to be the handsomest of husbands, and the youngest at heart."

He put his arm around her waist and drew her down beside him.

"I have decided that grief carried to excess is a selfish emotion," he said. "My mother's legacy is love and the capacity for making others happy. Allowing myself to wallow in grief would be to distort her memory and dishonor her legacy."

"And what brought you to this decision?" Elsie asked, for she knew that the change in her husband could not have been easily won.

"A scrap of embroidery," he said softly. "It was a piece she left unfinished. I saw it, and I realized that I, too, am unfinished. I have the choice now of holding onto my sorrow and remaining incomplete or of moving forward in the way Mamma would want for me. Look at how blessed I am. I have the most wonderful wife in the world, a beautiful child, and another coming soon. I have Ion and more than a hundred people here who depend on me. And I have my God, who bids me to drink at His bottomless well of love and strength. With all these gifts, I would be a foolish man to allow my heart to turn cold with grief."

"You could never be a foolish man, my dearest," Elsie said, hugging him. "Grief is part of God's plan for us."

"I agree. The ability to grieve is a necessary part of us. But God gives us choices, and I have chosen not to indulge my grief at the expense of others. I will cherish the memory of my mother as you cherish yours. But I will not retreat from life."

Life was very much on Elsie's mind as the time for her second confinement approached. Dr. Barton had estimated that the baby would be born in early May, but little Edward Horace Travilla decided to make an early appearance and so was an April baby.

Elsie's Troubled Times

Like his older sister, he was pronounced healthy and fit upon arrival, though perhaps a little smaller than expected. Unlike Missy, however, the new infant was a noisy fellow from the start. He was never hesitant to bellow for what he wanted, and for his first three or four months, he kept the entire household at Ion on the run.

"Too loud!" exclaimed Missy one morning. She had come to her parents' room, as she did every morning, for their prayers before breakfast, and they had just said "Amen" when the baby set off one of his alarms.

Lifting her screaming, hungry infant from the cradle, Elsie hurried through a side door into her dressing room. With comic gravity, Missy covered her ears with her hands and scrunched her face into a grimace. Edward took her onto his knee and gently removed her hands from her head. "He's just a baby, and all babies cry. That is what babies do," the amused father explained.

"Why?" asked Missy, who was now close to her second birthday and becoming curious about everything.

"Because babies can't tell us what they want in words. They cry when they are hungry or wet or cold or when they want to be held," Edward said, bouncing Missy gently. "You cried when you were a baby, though not so loudly or often as Eddie, I admit. Aren't you glad that you can use words now?"

"Yes, Papa," Missy said thoughtfully, "but Eddie hurts my ears."

Edward laughed. "Mine as well, sometimes, though your Mamma would not like to hear us say so. But Eddie will get over it soon."

"Papa, Eddie is a pretty baby," Missy said, trying to balance her complaint with a pleasantry.

"I think so, too," Edward agreed at he set his daughter down from his knee.

"But loud," she added firmly, and at just that instant, another mighty yowl was heard through the door of the dressing room where Elsie was feeding her son. Edward laughed heartily and took Missy by the hand.

"What do you say we go down to our breakfast," he suggested. "Mamma will join us in a little while."

When they entered the dining room, they found a familiar figure waiting there.

"Grampa!" Missy cried in glee and ran across the room to be scooped up in Horace's arms. She covered his face with soft kisses and then reached for the spectacles that he now used.

"Can I wear?" she asked.

"Yes, you may, child, but only for a moment," Horace replied. "The lenses are strong, and we don't want to harm your beautiful eyes."

So Missy carefully took the glasses from her grandfather and just as carefully propped them across her nose.

"You look funny, Grampa," she laughed, staring close into his face.

"Without my spectacles, pet, everything looks a bit funny to me too," he said.

"Elsie will be down in a few minutes," Edward said, "as soon as the baby is fed."

"How is my grandson?" Horace asked. "Is he gaining weight as he should?"

"He is," Edward said cheerfully. "I tell you, Horace, if the rest of him is just half as strong as his voice, our namesake will grow up with the strength of a Samson. Missy, give the spec-tacles back to your grandfather. Horace, will you share breakfast with us?"

"I ate before leaving The Oaks. But I will have coffee and perhaps one of Lavinia's delicious corn muffins."

Horace gently placed his granddaughter in her high-seated chair and took a place beside her at the table.

"And what will you be eating this morning?" he asked, leaning toward the child with an expression of intense interest.

Elsie's Troubled Times

Missy raised a chubby fist and at each item she named, she raised a finger—"Bread . . . honey . . . berries . . . milk."

"Those are four good things for little girls to eat," Horace said, and he slowly counted each of her fingers aloud for her: "One . . . two . . . three . . . four."

Missy gazed at her fingers as if some magic secret had just been revealed to her.

"You are a born teacher, Papa," said Elsie from the doorway. "I believe that it is your greatest pleasure." She came forward and kissed her Papa first, then Edward—both of whom stood at her entrance—before taking her seat.

"Poor Trip might not agree with you today," Horace said, resuming his place. "He has been struggling with some advanced mathematical problems which he knows he must master if he is to attend the military academy at West Point."

"So he still wants to be a soldier?" Edward asked. Elsie thought she detected the faint hint of concern in his voice, though Horace noticed nothing.

"He has never wanted anything else. I am afraid that I cannot convince him to attend our old alma mater, Edward, nor will I try. The military academy is his goal, and I believe he will achieve it."

"But what of—" Edward started to say, but broke off his sentence. "No. We should speak of these things later, when little ones are busy elsewhere."

"Tell us how everyone is at The Oaks," Elsie said, changing the subject. "Has Rosie fully recovered from her chicken pox?"

"She is about over it, though a few of the spots still linger. But she is well enough to become quite angry with me whenever I tease and call her Dotty."

This remark sent little Missy into a fit of giggles, and breakfast proceeded in a happy, family way.

CHAPTER

5

Rumors of War

"You will hear of wars and rumors of wars, but see to it that you are not alarmed. Such things must happen, but the end is still to come."

MATTHEW 24:6

fter Mrs. Travilla's death, the family demonstrated their respect for their loved one by refraining from attending all but the most important functions outside Ion. The birth of a second baby also freed them from normal social obligations. But work continued unabated. Edward ran the plantation with the same careful management that had always been his habit. He also assumed a good deal of the responsibility for Elsie's far-flung business interests, including Viamede, so it was he who made the necessary journey alone to Louisiana that summer. Not that Elsie had stepped aside. No, she kept herself fully involved in her business matters, but she was now the mother of a lively two-year-old and a new infant, as well as the mistress of Ion. It was extremely important to her that the house and its people should continue to operate with the same efficiency as they had under her beloved Mother Travilla. For Elsie and Edward, work proved to be a healing antidote for their grief.

There was a brief but frightening episode at The Oaks in the spring: first Trip and then little Rosie Dinsmore came down with scarlet fever — that most dreaded of contagious diseases which claimed the lives of so many children. Trip and Rosie were confined at The Oaks for the duration, and there were no visits between the Dinsmores and the Travillas while there was any possibility of transmitting the disease to the young Travillas. The Lord's blessing was on both houses in that crisis, however, for Trip and Rosie recovered with no ill effects and little Missy and Eddie were untouched by the danger.

"I think that the loss of one's child must be the hardest of all tragedies for a mother and father to bear," Rose was saying one Saturday afternoon late in June as she and Elsie sat on Ion's shaded veranda. She spoke in a quiet tone, but her words made Elsie clutch her own precious baby more closely to her breast. Both women were gazing at the other children playing on the lawn. Trip and his little sister Rosie were teaching Missy to play London Bridge, and Missy had collapsed in a bout of giggles after she was "captured" by her adored aunt and uncle.

"If a child is taken, it is God's will. But I must tell you, Elsie, that when Trip and Rosie were so ill, I would gladly have exchanged places with them and gone happily to my final rest. To see them healthy and laughing again, well"—her voice caught for an instant in the power of her emotion— "I can only thank our dear Heavenly Father for His infinite mercy and compassion. I think of other mothers who have been less fortunate and . . . ." Her comments trailed away.

"I wish I could have been at The Oaks to help you, Mamma," Elsie said earnestly. She had observed that Rose, unlike the children, had not yet regained her full strength after the long weeks of caring for her youngsters. There was still a faint paleness in her complexion and slowness in her movements—not noticeable except to those who loved her best— that spoke of weariness. But when she smiled, as she did now, the familiar Rose was clearly still present.

"You would have been a great comfort to me and your father, dear, but we would have done nothing to separate you from your wee ones or put them in any danger."

"But you nursed Trip and Rosie day and night. Now you deserve a rest, Mamma," Elsie continued. "None of us will be able to take our usual summer holiday this year, but have you considered visiting your family in Philadelphia? I know the children would enjoy seeing their grandparents, and I'm sure a change of scene would be good for you and Papa. Your mother would love to pamper you for a while," she added with a little laugh.

"We have decided to do just that," Rose said. "We will go to my parents for all the month of October. Horace does not feel he can stay the full time, but he will go with us, and we plan to celebrate our wedding anniversary there."

"Oh, what a good plan!" Elsie said excitedly. "My gracious, how that glorious day comes back to me as if it were yesterday. Can it really have been fourteen years since your wedding day? You seem hardly a minute older than you were when you became my Mamma and brought me so much love and happiness."

Rose laughed. "You flatter me, dear Elsie. I have aged as I should, and do you know I have acquired my first gray hairs."

"Then you have hidden them artfully, Mamma, for I can see no hint of gray," Elsie replied honestly. "Papa, on the other hand, has grown quite a crop and becomes more and more like Grandpa in appearance. I fear that I am responsible for a good many of his gray hairs."

"A very few, dear Elsie. Horace has always valued his gray hair, for he says that each one represents a lesson learned or a hurdle crossed in life. But do you not think he looks distinguished?"

"I do, indeed. Perhaps he needs the gray hair, since his face is still so youthful."

The two women chatted on in this pleasant way for some time. It was good for Rose, and for Elsie as well, to put aside weighty concerns for a time, and Rose seemed to walk with a quicker step when they went to supper that evening.

But as the year moved forward, such moments of peaceful respite became less and less frequent. The world outside the busy routines of Ion and The Oaks was full of strife, and no one could escape the growing conflict between North and South.

⁓

Rose and her children were just ending their stay with the Allisons, and Horace had already returned to the South when news came that was to alter forever the lives of all.

Elsie's Troubled Times

In mid-October, a man named John Brown had been captured and sentenced to death for treason after a failed attempt to seize the United States arsenal at Harper's Ferry in Virginia. Brown's goal had been to take the weapons there, flee into the mountains, and launch an armed rebellion among the slaves.

"Look at this!" Horace exclaimed one morning as he stormed into the library at Ion where Edward and Elsie were going over some reports from Viamede. Horace was waving a New York newspaper that he tossed on the desk before his daughter and son-in-law.

"Read the editorial," he commanded. And they did, as Horace paced the room.

"Everyone knows that Brown is insane, but I fear he has lit the fuse that will destroy our nation," Horace said in exasperation. "In the North, he has become a martyr to the abolitionist cause. See how they honor him! And here in the South, he is the worst nightmare—a man who would end slavery with guns and bloodshed. I fear all hope of peaceful compromise will die when he goes to the gallows."

Horace slumped into a chair beside the fire. Elsie slipped briefly from the room to find Old Joe and call for coffee. When she returned to the library, Edward was saying, "But there is still hope. With the election of a new President next year perhaps—"

Horace cut him off. "My old friend, you have always been the more rational of us, but I fear the time for reason is fast slipping away. You know the politicians as well as I do, and you know that men of moderation have lost their voice in the halls of power. The extremists of both sides are in control. No President, however much goodwill he possesses, will be able to mediate now. North and South, lines are being drawn."

"If you are correct—and for once, I pray God that you are not—then we will soon be required to choose a side, and that I am unwilling to do," Edward said in his calm manner. "I must believe that compromise is still possible. You know that I would gladly give all the slaves on this plantation their freedom at this very moment to preserve our great nation."

"I, too," Horace said in a milder tone, "but it would be an empty gesture and one that would end any influence we might have among our neighbors. The South depends upon slavery for survival. Our fortunes are built upon it! Yet how I wish this evil system had never been thrust upon us. Slavery is wrong — a sin against man and God!"

"Mother knew that," Elsie interjected. "That is why she freed Lavinia, the only slave who was her own, and asked forgiveness on her death bed. If we follow Mother's example and do the same here and at Viamede, I am certain we would prosper under a system of employment rather than servitude. Would that not have some good influence upon others?"

"On a very few, I'm afraid," Edward said thoughtfully. "To most we would be seen as traitors to the South and its cause. We are in a moral cleft now. To free our slaves is the right and godly choice, yet to do so would endanger not only us but also our slaves themselves. A free slave in the South today is in constant jeopardy. The bounty hunters snatch them off the streets and sell them back into servitude while the law looks in the other direction."

A knock at the door silenced him. Old Joe entered, bearing a tray which he set upon a low table near the fireplace.

"Can I get you folks anything else?" he asked. "Lavinia's got some right nice buns left over from breakfast."

"No, but thank you, Joe," Elsie said politely. "Coffee is all we need at present."

Joe, who had sensed the mood in the room, moved swiftly to the door and left without another word. He may not have known what was being said, but he knew that trouble was brewing. All of the slaves had heard of John Brown's rebellion in Virginia. Some welcomed the news, but others were fearful of its meaning. Everyone, however, felt that change was in the wind, and no one knew what direction it would take.

This was but the first of many discussions to take place at Ion and The Oaks over the next weeks and months. Horace talked often to his father as well, and other planters in the area. But he quickly learned to keep his doubts and moderate views to himself in their company. Passion was rapidly replacing reason in every corner. White Southerners of all classes felt deeply abused and misunderstood by the North. They demanded the right to work out their own problems, and many still believed that slavery would die out naturally, if they were left to their own devices. Pride played its role, too.

"This country depends on the South," old Mr. Dinsmore angrily declared to his son during one of their visits. "Why, our cotton sales saved them during the Panic of '57! Yet they would destroy us with their tariffs and Abolition! The time is fast coming, Son, when we must stand up for ourselves and claim our rightful position."

"To the point of secession, Father?" Horace asked cautiously.

"Secession if need be," Horace, Sr., replied with conviction.

"And war?"

The old man hesitated for a moment before answering.

"War is an evil thing, my boy, but sometimes necessary. We fought the British twice for our independence, and no men were braver in those conflicts than the sons of the South. I do not want war, Horace, but I will support it if I must to preserve our honor and our way of life."

"What of Arthur and Walter?"

"They will do what must be done," the old man said with certainty, "as will my sons-in-law."

"Do you include Edward Allison in that remark?" Horace asked deferentially.

Rumors of War

The old man paused again. "I had not thought of Edward,"
he said. His tone had changed. The bluster was gone—
replaced, Horace thought, by an uncharacteristic sadness.

"The Allisons have been good friends for so many years, and
we became family when you married Rose and then Adelaide
wed her Edward. Why, Mr. Allison has been my friend since
before you were born, Horace. Yet in this conflict, we are at
opposite poles. Still, I cannot imagine sending my boys to fight
against the husband of my daughter and the sons of my old
friend."

"Then let us pray that day never comes, Father," Horace
said gently.

"And yet it may," Mr. Dinsmore said slowly. Suddenly
Horace saw that pain and age had replaced the anger in his
father's face.

"Brother against brother," the old man said softly. "It may
come to that yet."

Time marched inexorably forward, and with it, the division
between North and South grew into a chasm. When the country elected its sixteenth President in the fall of 1860, it seemed
the end of hope had come for the great Union. Abraham
Lincoln, the candidate of the Republican Party and a man who
sought peaceful compromise, won not even a majority of the
people's votes—receiving no votes from the deepest parts of the
South. But after a divisive campaign that divided the rival
party, Lincoln led the three other candidates. When he took the
oath of office on March 4, 1861, the United States was no
longer united.

Soon after Lincoln's election, the state of South Carolina
had voted to separate itself from the Union and was followed
within six weeks by Georgia, Florida, Alabama, Mississippi,

and Louisiana. Together, these six had declared themselves to be the independent Confederate States of America in February of 1861. Still, men of goodwill pursued some solution that would bring the Union together again. In his final days as President, James Buchanan denied the right of the Confederate states to secede but also vowed not to use force against them. Other Southern states refused to join their sister states in separating, hoping that the threat of succession would force the new President to make concessions to their demands. But there could be no compromise on slavery. Abraham Lincoln, who had not sought to abolish slavery in the South, nevertheless refused to allow the United States Constitution to be amended so that slavery might be controlled entirely by the states and spread into the West. The President in his inaugural address disavowed force and held out the olive branch to the South, calling upon all sides to hear the "better angels of our nature" and restore the Union.

As it happened, the Travillas and the Dinsmores were in the house of Rose's parents in Philadelphia on Inauguration Day, and they eagerly read the reports of Lincoln's speech in the newspapers.

"It is a simple speech," Rose commented.

"Yet eloquent in its simplicity," Horace said. "I know the South has no love for this man from Illinois, but perhaps he can build a peaceful compromise and reconcile both sides, if they will listen."

"What is this president of the Confederacy like—this Jefferson Davis?" asked Edward Allison who, with Adelaide, had joined the family that evening.

"Not, as you have probably been told, one of the rabid hotheads," Edward Travilla replied. "I always thought him a rational man, and his voice was often raised for compromise. Yet he believes in the Southern cause with all his heart. Do you know that he and Abraham Lincoln were born near one another in Kentucky? I do not know now if they share much else, but they do share a homeland."

"I am so torn," Adelaide exclaimed emotionally. "I love my beautiful South and feel that she has been greatly imposed upon by the North. Yet I cannot help feeling she is in the wrong. Papa writes so angrily about the South being held in chains and forced into servitude by the North, yet he sees not that he exists by the servitude of others—oh, it would be comic if it were not so tragic."

"Dear Wife," Edward Allison said, coming to sit at her side. "I believe that many of your fellow Southerners, your father among them, have been misled by their politicians. They have been inflamed by these cries of states' rights, and they are acting from fear and anger rather than reason."

"Do not be so quick to think of Southerners as sheep led to the slaughter," Edward Travilla said. "It is true we have our share of rabble-rousers, as you do here. But were it not for the single issue of slavery, I believe my neighbors—both the rich and the poor—would bend to compromise. You understand industry, my friend. You have become an industrialist yourself, a producer as well as a seller of goods. But in the South, you would be a rare commodity. You will find no great factories there. At home, we are a land of farmers, some as large as Horace and I, but most small. The farmer of the South believes—and he may well be correct—that when slavery goes, it will be the end of his way of life. He is not so stupid as to be led about by the few Judas goats among our politicians. But he is afraid that the only life he has ever known, the life of his father and grandfathers and great-grandfathers, is about to be swallowed up by forces he cannot control. The Southerner's heart and soul are bred in the land, and rightly or wrongly, he sees the rest of the nation ready to rob him of his one possession and his ability to make a life for himself and his children. Were the positions reversed, I believe you might react as he has."

"And do you feel so?" Edward Allison asked with real concern.

Edward Travilla smiled ruefully and replied, "No, I do not. If slavery were abolished tomorrow, I should fall down upon my knees and thank our Heavenly Father for His deliverance, as He once delivered the Jews from Egypt. To me, as your Adelaide has said, slavery itself is the cruelest kind of shackle on those who suffer from it and those who impose it upon others. I believe that the South must change, must seek a balance between the old ways and the new. I do not believe that the land will be lost to us, nor the best aspects of our way of life wiped away like chalk on a slate. I have faith that, given time, the South can adapt to and even welcome change. My great fear is of the consequences of having change forced upon us. It may be necessary, but the outcome will be worse than anyone anticipates."

"Would you fight for the South?" Mrs. Allison asked, casting worried eyes at Horace, her Southern son-in-law.

"I cannot bear to answer that question," Horace replied. "Edward has expressed my position better than I could myself. Yet should either side be foolish enough to take up arms, I do not know where my loyalty would fall. In this matter, I do not pray for myself or my loved ones, but for the preservation of our Union itself. I love the South, but I love the Union more. I do not believe that either can win in an armed conflict, though one or the other be victorious. I only hope that when we return to these United States, they will be united once more, and no choices will be required."

That return, the Dinsmores and Travillas expected, would be within four months. At the beginning of the new year, they had decided to travel to Europe once again. Several pressing business matters had arisen that required both Horace and Edward to meet with their European agents and the cotton buyers of Paris and London. Soon afterwards, Horace had received a letter from one of Mrs. Murray's nieces informing him that the elderly lady was suffering from a terminal illness. The doctors expected Mrs. Murray to live for another year or two, but the end was inevitable. Mrs. Randall, who had penned the letter, only wanted to tell Mr. Dinsmore of the situation and to invite him, Elsie, Mr. Travilla, and any of their family to come to Edinburgh should they visit England. "It would give my beloved aunt the greatest delight to behold your faces once more," Mrs. Randall said, "while it is still possible."

Elsie, who corresponded with Mrs. Murray regularly and had been given no hint of an illness, was adamant. She would accompany Edward on the voyage and the children must go as well. Rose, too, was anxious to travel. She had not fully recovered her strength from the events of the past two years — the death of her dear friend Mrs. Travilla, the illnesses of her children, and the constant worry about the possibility of a conflict that could rend her family apart — and she believed that the sea voyage followed by the delightful sights of England would be curative. (In her heart, Rose nursed another fear that she expressed to no one, not even Horace. It was for Trip, so young and headstrong like his father. The boy had always wanted to be a soldier. But if war did come? The thought of losing her son to the battlefields was almost more than she could bear.)

Thus it had been agreed that both families would travel across the Atlantic. They were to depart Philadelphia in several days and sail from New York at the beginning of April. Their return was planned for the following August. But even the best laid plans, as the Scots' poet has said, often go astray.

CHAPTER

6

The
Opening Shot

"From now on there will be five in one family divided against each other, three against two and two against three."

LUKE 12:52

The Opening Shot

On the families' arrival at their London hotel, one of Horace's first actions was to purchase the newspapers of the day. As he read, a look of horror came to his face, and he had to struggle to compose himself before rejoining his happy party. Everyone was so busy sorting the luggage and seeing that the carriage drivers and hotel staff had correct instructions that no one except Edward noticed the strained look in Horace's eyes.

Edward managed to take Horace aside and ask in a hushed voice, "What has happened, my friend?"

"They have done it," Horace said in disgust and handed the newspaper to Edward. "Until this moment, I honestly believed that a solution could be found, but the first shots have been fired, and our own beloved state has joined the Confederacy."

Edward read the report hastily. Indeed, Fort Sumter, a garrison of the United States near Charleston in South Carolina, had been bombarded and occupied by the forces of the Confederacy. The states of Virginia, North Carolina and Arkansas had left the Union to become part of the Confederacy, and Tennessee was expected to join soon.

"Lincoln has called on the Northern states to supply militia to put down the rebellion," Horace said in a low voice, "and in both North and South, men are rallying to the call for volunteers."

"Look here," Edward said, pointing to an article in another of the newspapers Horace had bought. "President Lincoln has put Baltimore under federal control. It seems he is trying to keep any further states from taking the step of secession. I did not believe it would come so soon, my friend. Until this moment, I retained my hope that reason would prevail," he concluded sadly.

Elsie's Troubled Times

"I think we should keep this to ourselves until we have settled into the hotel," Horace said quickly, for he had noticed Rose and Elsie looking around the crowded hotel lobby for their husbands. "Let us give our loved ones an hour more of peace."

Despite the men's best efforts, both Elsie and Rose sensed that something was wrong. Upon reaching their suites, they quickly put Chloe, Dinah, and Old Joe in charge of the children and the unpacking. Then they joined their husbands in the Dinsmores' parlor.

Rose spoke first: "I fear that the news from home is bad."

"It is, my dear," Horace replied, crossing the elegant room to stand at her side. "Fort Sumter has been bombarded and surrendered to the Confederacy. It was not much of a victory, as the Union troops had been weakened by a blockade. Yet it has fanned the flames of Southern pride, and three more states have seceded, our own among them."

A little gasp escaped Elsie, who had gone to sit with Edward on the couch. She grabbed his hand. "Then they are at war?" she asked.

"Not officially, dearest," Edward replied. "At least, not yet. It will take time to assemble armies on both sides. There may yet be hope of settlement, but very little hope, I'm afraid."

"What shall we do?" Rose inquired urgently. "Should we consider an immediate return to our homes?"

"No, I do not think that is necessary," Horace said slowly. "The business that Edward and I have here is exceedingly important and cannot be concluded for several weeks. During that time we can decide our best course."

"I want to know all that is happening," Elsie said in a firm voice. Edward rose and went to a table where the newspapers lay. He brought them to his wife, and she began reading the accounts.

The Opening Shot

"We must tell the children," Rose said, looking anxiously into Horace's eyes. "Even here in the safety of London, they will soon enough learn of what is going on at home. Little Missy and Eddie are too young to understand, but Trip and Rosie must be told. I cannot allow them to hear this dreadful news from anyone other than ourselves."

"We shall talk to them this very afternoon," Horace assured her.

Their conversation with Trip and Rosie took place as Horace promised. Both children were deeply concerned for the welfare of their loved ones at home.

"Will they fight, Papa?" Trip demanded. "I mean Uncle Edward and Richard and Daniel and Fred in the North, and Uncle Arthur and Uncle Walter in the South. Will they take sides against each other?"

"I cannot tell you for certain, Son," Horace replied, "but they are all loyal to their causes."

"Will my uncles be soldiers, Mamma?" young Rosie asked with tears in her eyes. "Will they be killed?"

Rose hugged her daughter close. "Oh, my darlings, we must pray very hard that they are all spared to us, no matter what happens. We must ask our Heavenly Father to watch over them and protect them in the midst of this strife."

Trip was pacing the floor, as his father had done so often in times of worry. "Is Uncle Daniel still in Central America? If so, he will be safe there. But the others?" He cast his father a beseeching look. "You know they are on opposite sides, Papa. What will they do?"

Looking into his son's face, Horace felt more helpless than he had since that day many years ago when Elsie lay at the brink of death. He struggled for a moment to make his voice steady and strong, then he said, "I do not know what they will do. We must await word from home. Trip, it is hard to wait, I know. But we must. We cannot allow ourselves to imagine what we do not know."

"I wish I could be there, Papa!" Trip declared in a burst of emotion.

"But what would you do, Son?" Horace replied evenly. "Could you choose a side for yourself?"

The question clearly troubled Trip. He dropped into a chair. His arms fell loosely at his sides, and his long legs stretched out before him. His face clouded as he thought. After some moments, he said, "No, Papa, I could not choose. I love my home, my state, my South. Yet you and Mamma have always taught me how precious is the Union that binds all the states together, and I believe you have taught me right. If I were there, I might know what to do, but how can anyone choose between the things he loves best?"

"Then let us pray, all of us, that the choice is not necessary. There is still time for mending. Let us pray together now that God will help our leaders to find a path that does not lead to open war. Let us ask our Lord and Savior to heal over the deep wounds that divide our people and our nation and to bring an end to this conflict before another life is lost."

And so, led by Horace, they all knelt and lifted their earnest prayers for peace and for the protection of their great country and its people on all sides.

⚬

By the end of their first week in London, they had received the news they awaited. They had hoped the word would be good, but expected less. When two letters arrived, they confirmed expectations.

Mrs. Allison had written from Philadelphia. Sophie's letter came from Ashlands, the Carringtons' plantation. Rose read her mother's letter aloud to her husband, Elsie, and Edward who had gathered in the parlor after breakfast. It was full of the sad tidings of what was happening in general, but Mrs. Allison had carefully avoided explicit news of her sons. (In truth, the lady could not yet bring herself to contemplate the impact war might have on her family.) One exception, however, was heartening. Edward Allison would not be enlisting. He had been told by the Secretary of War himself that industry must be kept going. Edward would be expected to stay at his factory and continue to direct the production of supplies. "Edward is working day and night to meet the Army's needs, and we hardly see him, but at least he and dear Adelaide are safe with us," Mrs. Allison had concluded.

When Rose came to the second letter, from her beloved sister Sophie, tears began to roll slowly down her cheeks, though she kept her voice under control. The words on the page were heartrending:

"Dearest Rose,

"I think I shall go crazy. Harry has enlisted in the Confederate Army. And Mamma has written that Richard and Fred are intent upon enlisting for the Union. Daniel is finally coming home from Central America and I'm sure he plans to join. What if they should all someday meet in battle? My husband against my brothers! I cannot think of it without weeping.

"I have argued with Harry, for I cannot see the meaning of any of this. But he is furious with the North. He believes with all his heart that the South is being oppressed and robbed of its freedom of choice. He says that the South's secession is no less a demand for freedom than our American Revolution in 1776. He tries to assure me and soothe my tears by telling me that the North will not wage war. But I know he's wrong!

Elsie's Troubled Times

I know my brothers and their friends. They will fight for the Union — to the last man if need be!

"Arthur and Walter Dinsmore were here yesterday, and Arthur is determined to go to the Confederate Army as quickly as he can. Walter said little, however, and seems not to share this fever for battle. While Harry and Arthur had gone to look at the horses, I had a chance to question Walter. I believe him to be deeply torn. The pressure upon him to enlist must be very strong, especially from Arthur and his parents.

"Dear Rose, how can this thing have happened? What has brought us to this point? For reasons you must understand, I am glad you are not here. You must stay in England and guard your family against this insanity. Pray for us. Pray for us all."

"Your loving sister, Sophie"

As Rose ended her reading, Horace jumped up from his chair and began to pace.

"Sophie is right," he exclaimed. "It is lunacy to wage civil war!"

"But the newspapers say it cannot last long, Papa," Elsie interjected. "They say three months at most."

"The newspapers are wrong, dear Daughter," Horace replied forcefully. "I hope the papers are correct in their predictions, but in my heart I know this will be no ordinary war."

Elsie looked quizzically at her husband.

"I fear your father is right," Edward said. "This is American against American, and neither side will be easily defeated. I might be more hopeful if it were a battle against a foreign invader."

"If it is over in three *years*, I shall be much surprised," Horace added with great sadness. "We must prepare ourselves to wait out a long and bitter conflict. When we next see our homeland, all will be changed forever. Men may have their wars, but none are ever ready for its consequences."

⁓

After much discussion, the Dinsmores and the Travillas made their decision to remain overseas for at least another six months. Letters continued to arrive from home, each one more frightening than the last.

Horace Dinsmore, Sr., wrote Horace a letter superficially full of Southern bluster and pride. But between the lines, Horace could sense the stress in his father's words. The old man wrote of the South's noble cause, the bravery of its fighting forces, the determination of those left at home to keep the Army well supplied and to hold spirits high. He praised Arthur's decision to volunteer, described his departure with the regiment raised by Harry Carrington. He even had good words for Dick Percival, Enna's husband and an early recruit to the Confederate forces. But of Walter, Mr. Dinsmore said only that his youngest son was attending to affairs at The Oaks and Ion and that both plantations were running well.

A shorter letter from Enna confirmed Horace's suspicions:

"Mamma and Papa are outraged at Walter, and I can't blame them a bit," Enna had written. *"My Dick joined up the day after Fort Sumter fell, and now Arthur has gone off. I am so proud of them, and they looked so handsome in their gray uniforms. How can Walter be such a laggard? He spends most of his time at The Oaks, and when we do see him, he mopes around all gloomy. Mamma confronted him the other day. I wish you could have seen her. She was near livid with anger, and I thought she might have an attack. She came*

close to denouncing him as a traitor, and she did call him a Yankee. Right to his face! But Walter didn't argue back, just like he never stood up for himself when we were children. He says that he hasn't decided what to do. He told her that he would not fight until he was ready to face death and judgment, whatever that means. Mamma said that he wouldn't fight because he's gotten himself engaged to a Yankee girl and she's poisoned his mind. I really don't know what is wrong with Walter. Mamma is ready to toss him out, and last week Papa threatened to disinherit him if he didn't take his stand with the Confederacy. They had a talk, and I don't know what was said, but Papa has told us to leave Walter be for the time being. Papa says he'll come around, but I will believe that when I see him march off under the banner of the Confederacy!"

A month after Enna's letter, another arrived from Roselands. It was to be one of the last that the Dinsmores and the Travillas were to receive from the South. President Lincoln had ordered a blockade of the Confederate coast, and it had become increasingly difficult and dangerous for any ship to leave Southern ports. The letter-writer had entrusted the missive to a friend who was secretly traveling north to join the Union Army. When this man reached the nation's capital, he handed the letter to another friend who was traveling to Delaware to see his wife one last time. Eventually, the letter was put aboard a British ship and transported across the ocean to London. It was delivered to Mrs. Edward Travilla.

"Dear Elsie,
"I can only pray that this letter will reach you, and if it does, please share it with Horace, and Edward and Rose as

well. I have addressed it to you because as I prepare to face the unknown, I feel the need to thank you for a gift you may not know you once gave me.

"When we were children, I used to believe that you possessed secret abilities that the rest of us lacked. I would watch when Arthur teased you so dreadfully and my mother was so unkind to you, and during that time when Horace came back and was so unfair to you. You would cry, as anyone would, and I knew how miserable you felt inside because that was how I felt whenever I was frightened or angry. But I could not understand how you always returned with a smile and kind words for your tormentors. Even when I was just eight or nine years old, I sensed that you had some secret source of strength. I knew that you were a Christian in a way that my mother and father did not approve, but it has taken me many years to learn that your 'secret' is available to all, if they open their hearts to the love and forgiveness of our Lord and Savior. Without your knowing it, Elsie, you pointed me in the right direction by your example. For that I shall be grateful to you always.

"I used to worry because I was so unlike the rest of my family. Each of them, even Horace, seemed so sure of themselves, while I was shy and, yes, cowardly. I shall never forget the time when Jim was accused of taking Papa's gold watch. It was only when you spoke up and told the truth that Jim was saved from an unjust and cruel punishment. I remember that it was very hard for you, that you didn't want to tell on Arthur. I lied to Papa because I was afraid; you told the truth even though you were afraid. I remember thinking to myself, 'Elsie is as scared as I am, but she is doing what is right while I've done wrong.'

Elsie's Troubled Times

"*I am afraid now, Elsie. Afraid of going to war, of dying, and worse, of bringing death to others. But because I have given myself into the hands of our Loving Father, I can face the fear and do my duty. These past months, I have searched for answers. Honestly, I cannot tell you that I know my decision is correct, but I will join the Confederates because, like my father, I love this land and will do what I can to prevent its devastation. I do not accept that our Southern cause is entirely just, but I'm going in the hope that a show of forceful determination will be enough to convince the Union to seek peaceful resolution.*

"*Arthur returned home this morning. He is now a captain, and I will join his regiment. We leave Roselands at dawn. I go in the knowledge that whatever comes, I am washed in the blood of Jesus Christ. I have received His pardon, and all my faith is in Him now and for eternity. I find my comfort and guidance in His Holy Scriptures, and I trust Him to lead me along His path.*

"*I wish I had been able to share my thoughts with you before you left for England, but you know that I was always solitary in my ways. There is one who has helped me along this journey to faith. Her name is Grace, and she is from New Jersey. I met her one summer when we were on holiday at Cape May. We became engaged in April, not long before the fall of Fort Sumter, and I have no chance of seeing her again soon. Promise me, dear niece, that should I not survive, you will make contact with her some day and tell her how much I loved her. I think you have much in common, beginning with your faith in the redeeming love of Christ. Seek her out for me, if need be.*

"*The morning is coming fast, and I must go now. But one last word. Stay where you are while this conflict lasts. Convince Horace and Edward that they can play little role in* this war, but they will be greatly needed when peace comes. Whatever the outcome of this terrible division, the South will need strong men and women when peace is restored. Come back only when it is time to rebuild and renew.

"Kiss the children for me—even Trip who thinks himself too old for such nonsense. May God bless you all and watch over you now and forever."

"Your loving Uncle Walter"

CHAPTER

Reports and Regrets

"For the eyes of the Lord range throughout the earth to strengthen those whose hearts are fully committed to him."

2 CHRONICLES 16:9

*D*ays turned into weeks, weeks to months, and the families settled into new routines in London. They found a house in a fashionable section of the city, handsomely furnished and large enough to accommodate two families and their servants. Horace took a lease on the place, and by June they were well established in their temporary abode. With the help of old friends, Rose and Elsie had hired the necessary staff to run the house, including an excellent cook and a valet who served Horace and Edward. The men were often away during the day on business, though Horace never shirked his teaching duties, meeting for two hours each morning with Trip and Rosie. Elsie was naturally busy with her two little ones, and Rose was occupied with the running of the new household.

The Dinsmores and the Travillas, all of whom were remembered with much pleasure from their previous visits, were welcome arrivals on the London social scene, and soon old acquaintances began to call. Afternoon tea with guests, English style, became a routine in Quince House, as their home was called.

"I had not realized that we made so many friends when we were last here," Rose laughed one afternoon as she returned to the parlor after showing the last of a rather large group of ladies to their carriages. "Mrs. Bruxton is a delightful conversationalist, and her daughter is charming."

"Did I hear Mrs. Bruxton say that her daughter is to be presented to the Queen?" Elsie asked.

"In the fall. It is to be her formal coming-out season, I understand. Lady Catherine commented on your appearance, dear," Rose said with a smile.

"Oh, dear," Elsie sighed. "I hope I did nothing to offend her."

Elsie's Troubled Times

"Far from it. Lady Catherine said that she was amazed to learn that you are the mother of two young children. Her exact words were, 'Elsie looks not a day older than when I first laid eyes on her six years ago. She has the face and figure of a girl and is surely one of the loveliest exports we have received from the colonies.'"

Elsie blushed. "Lady Catherine is very sweet but rather elderly and perhaps in need of spectacles," she replied in a jesting tone. "Did she really say 'the colonies'?"

"She was but an infant when the Revolutionary War ended. It could be that she was never informed of the final outcome," Rose answered in an equally light tone. "I do not think her term unusual, however. I have noticed that many of our English friends refer to our great and sovereign nation as 'the colonies.' I believe it is simply a habit of speech rather than a deliberate insult."

Elsie, in a different mood now, sat upon a sofa and gazed dreamily out of a nearby window.

"Our English friends are all very kind to us, and visits with them are a welcome distraction," she said, "but I must admit that my thoughts are never far from home. It is strange, isn't it, that a conflict thousands of miles away can be such a constant presence. I think of everyone we love and what they are enduring now—I yearn to be with them, yet I know that we are fortunate to be here."

Rose came to the sofa and settled down beside Elsie. She took her daughter's hand and lightly patted it as she spoke. "I wait each day for letters from home, but I almost dread their arrival. All of my brothers, save Edward, now wear the uniform of our Union. Both of Horace's brothers and so many of our friends and their sons wear the gray. The danger to them all is with me every moment."

She squeezed Elsie's hand. "Might we not pray for their safe delivery?" she asked. "Just you and I?"

Reports and Regrets

"Yes, please," Elsie replied earnestly. "And let us pray for peace to be restored soon. If that is not possible, we must ask for the strength and courage to accept our Heavenly Father's will in all things."

Their hands clasped together, the two women bent their heads and raised their petitions to the One who hears all prayer.

News from home came in frustrating fits and starts. There would be days on end with no letter at all; then a bundle would arrive. Of course, the events from America were reported in the London newspapers, but these articles gave the larger picture—the political squabbles, the names of generals and the military preparations, the speeches of leaders from both North and South—not the personal accounts that Elsie and her family craved.

It was in July that the news arrived of the first major battle of the war. The Union was determined to drive southward and seize the Confederate capital in Richmond, Virginia. On July 16, 1861, some thirty-five thousand troops, under the command of General Irvin McDowell, had moved southwest from Washington toward a railroad center at Manassas Junction in Virginia. A smaller force of Confederate troops commanded by General P. G. T. Beauregard awaited reinforcements near a creek called Bull Run. The Union delayed, and the much-needed Confederate forces arrived. On July 21st, the armies met. The Union soldiers, mostly untrained in warfare, were disorganized and unprepared for the fierce Southern defense. Exhausted by the heavy fighting and confused about their orders, the Union attack fell apart, and the soldiers fled back to Washington in defeat.

Horace threw the newspaper on a table. It was several weeks after the Battle of Bull Run, and he had just read a detailed accounting in a New York paper that had arrived in the day's mail.

"I don't know what to feel," he exclaimed. "Should I see it as a victory or a defeat?"

"It is war, my friend," Edward said solemnly, "and it appears that the Union is as yet ill-prepared for such encounters. Almost a thousand killed. Thousands more wounded. Can it be regarded as anything but a defeat when so many lives are lost? From the accounts, it appears that the Confederates won on sheer willpower, for neither side possessed seasoned and war-hardened forces."

"At least Washington is safe, and there are no familiar names in the list of Union casualties," Horace said with a sigh. "Let us hope the same can be said for the Confederate side. That is a selfish thought, I know, but I cannot escape it."

"Selfish, perhaps, but altogether human."

More news did come. A letter arrived from Aunt Wealthy Stanhope. In her unique and cheerful style, that indomitable lady wrote of the preparations in Lansdale. Every house, she said, now proudly displayed the flag of the Union, and there had been a grand parade ("with marching banners and a red, white, and blue band") when the brave contingent of Lansdale volunteers had gone to the train to begin their journey to their training site. Miss Stanhope herself had organized a group of local ladies who knitted and sewed for the troops, and rolled bandages. ("A sad chore," she said, "when one thinks of how they will be put to use.") Wealthy's adored nephew, Harry Duncan, had enlisted soon after the fall of Fort Sumter and now served far away, near Washington:

"Harry writes that he is much impressed by the new leader of our forces, General McClellan. He, that is, Harry, says the training of the soldiers is going well and the men of our glorious Union will not again suffer a defeat like Bull Run. Do

*you remember my dear friend Dr. King, Lottie's father? He
has volunteered too. Doctors will be needed wherever battles
are fought. He leaves in a few days. I will be sick to see him
go. But then I can't be sick until he returns, can I? For no one
treats me so well when I am sick as Dr. King. Lottie finished
her college and is now in Philadelphia with an aunt. She,
Lottie that is, is teaching at a school there. Who would have
thought that girl had a head so full of brains?"*

A letter came the same day from May Allison. Though May
gave a graphic and colorful accounting of her great city's
preparations, her words could not conceal the sadness that all
the Allisons felt as they parted with Richard, Daniel, and Fred.
(*"We all put up a good front when they left. Now we work to keep ourselves from weeping. Everyone is busy at some job or another for the war
effort. It is hard to think of our dear Sophie, whom we cannot comfort
and hold close. Our prayers are with her always, for we know her heart
must be breaking to see her husband and her brothers on opposite
sides."*)

Some days later another letter was delivered, this addressed
to Elsie. She was alone in the library when Old Joe brought it to
her. She opened the thick envelope quickly, thinking it contained
news that she would share with the rest of the family. But as she
read, she understood why it had been sent to her. The letter, written in a swift, bold hand, was from Daniel Allison:

"Dear Elsie,

*"It is quiet here in camp now. Most of my comrades are
sleeping, for our training is arduous and goes from dawn to
dusk. But we are becoming an army now. No longer boys of
disparate interests and backgrounds, but a single unit of men
bound together by common purpose. When the fight comes, we
will be ready for it.*

Elsie's Troubled Times

"But, dear friend, I write to you not of the war, though the possibility of death in battle has impelled me to speak to you at last and to explain myself. How long ago was Sophie's wedding to Harry Carrington, yet I remember that time as vividly as if it were but hours past. It was the last time I saw your beautiful face, Elsie, in those weeks you and your family stayed in our home after your return from Europe. You were distracted, I recall. I believed you to be homesick for your South. But even though your thoughts were clearly elsewhere, mine were on you alone. What I could not admit then, I can tell you now. I was in love with you — I think I had loved you since we were children together that summer at Elmgrove — and I nursed in my heart the hope that you might return my feelings. When I learned that it could not be, that you were to marry Edward Travilla, I was, for a time, like a man gone mad.

"As I look back upon that time, I realize how beastly my behavior was. When my employer offered me the chance to manage his interests in Central America, I took it without hesitation. In my grief and longing, I trusted that great distance would dull my feelings. It did, eventually, but it was despicable of me to avoid my brother's wedding to Adelaide and then your own marriage to Mr. Travilla. Those terrible, cold notes that I wrote — what must you have thought of me? I have no excuse, save that I was like a person who has lost his lantern and must find his way in the darkness. I cut myself off from all that was dear to me — you and my family and friends. For a time, I even abandoned my faith. But God never abandoned me, and as time went on, I turned to Him with my sorrows. He showed me His Truth, and I was able to see that I had not lost you. I had almost lost myself. Love that does not want the happiness of the beloved is selfish. I love you still as my dearest friend, and I want for you the happiness you have found with your husband and your children.

"I have learned a powerful lesson, that love can change and that hearts can bend without breaking. My affection for you has not diminished, but its nature is altered. How I wish I could be talking to you in person at this moment, for then you could see that I am not being noble or self-sacrificing. God revealed to me that I have many purposes in this life. One of them is to be your true friend. Another was to return home when my country was threatened and to take up the cause of the Union. Still another is to be open-hearted so that when true love does come my way, I can welcome it in. This war cannot last forever, and perhaps when we meet again, I too will be happily married, and we will share stories of our children.

"My desire in writing to you was to ask your forgiveness for my actions and to mend any breach that may exist between us. If you want to give my letter to Mr. Travilla, please do so, for I owe you both this debt of honesty. Whatever comes in the struggle that lies ahead of us, I hope that both of you will always remember me as your true and faithful friend.

"I am enclosing a brief letter to Rose. Please watch over her for me. No sister was ever dearer than she."

"Daniel"

Elsie carefully removed the letter to Rose and laid it aside.

"Oh, dear Daniel," she sighed to herself as she folded the pages of her own message and returned them to the envelope. "How can you have thought there was a breach between us? I shall always be your friend."

Elsie's Troubled Times

She slipped Daniel's letter into a pocket of her skirt and went to the desk. Taking paper from the center drawer, she uncapped an ink bottle in the inkstand, found a pen, and began to write. Daniel had included the name of his regiment at the top of his letter. If she sent her letter off tomorrow, perhaps there was a chance it might reach him. Her words poured onto the creamy pages—her gratitude that he had felt free to write of his feelings, her assurances that she had never been offended by his actions, her relief that he was well, her thanks to God that He had brought her friend through his time of trial, and her joy in Daniel's strengthened faith and understanding. She wrote in a rush of good will, telling him plainly what was in her heart. She ended with the promise that they would all meet again, "perhaps beside the creek at Elmgrove where someday our children can dangle their bare feet in the cool water and sail their little ships made of sticks and leaves. Keep safe, my dear old friend."

That night, after she and Edward had checked on baby Eddie and then read Scripture and said prayers with Missy, Elsie bade her husband to come to their own room for a few moments before they rejoined Rose and Horace in the parlor. She took the letter from her pocket and gave it to her husband.

"It is from Daniel Allison," she said simply, "and he would like you to read it."

Seeing the seriousness in Elsie's face, Edward's immediate concern was that the letter contained news of misfortune. But as he read, he realized that it was both a confession and a plea for reconciliation.

"Poor chap," he said with a deep sigh. "Of course, I can understand his loving you. But to have suffered so much in isolation . . . . I doubt we could have been of help had we known the true motive for his years in Central America. But we can certainly assure him now that there is no ill feeling."

Reports and Regrets

"I wrote a reply," Elsie said. She took another envelope from her pocket and unfurled its contents. "I shall send it tomorrow so there may be a chance of its reaching Daniel before his regiment moves to another location. But I wanted you to read what I have written. Perhaps there is something I have left out."

She gave the pages to her husband and again he read.

Edward finished reading and then reached for his wife's hand, drawing her close. "No more words are needed, my darling. You have spoken with the eloquence of a true friend. And you have given us all something to look forward to—that day when we gather beside the creek together."

Elsie lay her head against his shoulder and said, "Do you think that day will come?"

"I pray that it will and soon. A day when all families will be reconciled and reunited," he replied. Then he added, "I think we should give your letter to Joe tonight, so he can deliver it by hand as soon as the sun rises. I learned just today of an American ship that sails for Boston in the morning. I know the captain. I will write a note to him asking that he get your letter into the right hands when he lands. Does that suit?"

"Oh, yes," Elsie said gladly. "Tell your captain friend that we wish him Godspeed and a safe voyage."

~

For the most part, the news and letters from home for the rest of that year told of a strange time compounded by busy preparation and terrible anxiety. Both the armies of the Union and the Confederacy had learned from Bull Run that they were not ready for the full-scale war some so eagerly sought. The Union was concentrating its efforts on building that army of trained fighting men of which Daniel had spoken and on shutting off all Confederate access to the sea. Union warships sailed down the eastern coast, seizing ports and tightening their blockade. To the west, General John C. Fremont established a strong Union force at Cairo, on the southern tip of Illinois, at the point where the Ohio River and the Mississippi River flow together. A new name appeared in the news reports — Ulysses S. Grant, the brigadier general who was given charge of Cairo.

The Confederates now had to protect their territory on two fronts. Troops under both flags were moved into Kentucky, and both sides faced one another, waiting for the orders that would come soon enough. The Union was preparing to push toward the Deep South, and the invasion could not be too far away.

The last letter from the South arrived late in the fall. It had been written from Viamede several months earlier. It came from Mr. Mason, the loyal chaplain who still guided his flock on Elsie's plantation. Edward read the letter aloud:

"Dear Mr. and Mrs. Travilla,

"I greatly fear this may be my last report to you for some time. I will be brief and to the point, though you know this is not my usual way.

"First, the plantation goes on much as you remember, and the war seems very far away from us. Only one change has threatened us in the least, and that is the loss of Mr. Spriggs. Being a New Englander and also possessing intense loyalty to his employers, he was greatly distressed by the loss of Fort Sumter and about where his own sympathies should come to rest. As you can guess, he said very little, but I could see a look in his eyes of great sadness and worry. He waited for a month, but near the end of May, he decided that his duty lay to the north. He would have stayed on until a new overseer could be employed, but with the threat of blockades, both Dr. Baliss (who has been of great assistance) and I encouraged Mr. Spriggs to make his departure while he could. We have

not heard from him, but I will assume that he completed the journey safely.

"Your attorney in New Orleans, Mr. Mayhew, promised to find a new manager as quickly as possible, but with so many men enlisting to fight, his task was not an easy one. I must report that until two weeks ago, I was left in charge. But thanks again to Dr. Baliss and to Mamie and to several of the veteran field and stable hands, Viamede progressed satisfactorily under my fragile leadership. Now we have a new manager hired by Mr. Mayhew. His name is Joshua McFee, and he is somewhat older than is normal for the position —fast approaching sixty, I estimate. But he is a good Christian with many years of experience, and his manner of exercising his authority coincides with all of your guidelines and expectations. His age is an advantage, for he cannot be called up to fight. Yet he is a fit man, and right glad to be working a large plantation again. He is married to a most industrious lady who has taken over the operation of the sewing room and is producing clothing for the soldiers as well as for Viamede's needs. I do not believe I have ever seen anyone pump the pedals of a sewing machine as fast as she. I believe she could power a steam-boat through desert sands! (Most fortunately, Aunt Mamie was happy to relinquish the responsibility of chief seam-stress. I briefly feared that I might have to mediate between the two women.) I help Mr. McFee when and how he needs me —without neglecting my spiritual duties, of course. Mr. Mayhew said that I should be the mule to Mr. McFee's plow. When I protested at his little joke, Mr. Mayhew explained kindly that he meant only that I have the strength of my youth while Mr. McFee has the wisdom of his age. In that *context, I am happy to serve as mule and to follow Mr. McFee's directions."*

Edward looked up. Horace was laughing, both Elsie and Rose were smiling brightly, and Trip was rolling on the floor while Missy and Rose stared at him with startled eyes.

"If this is brief," Trip managed to gasp out, "what does he consider to be lengthy?"

Edward shuffled through the fat sheaf of papers in his hand.

"Why, Trip, we have just begun," Edward said with mock stiffness. "Now if you can get control of yourself, little brother, I shall continue."

Trip sat up, took a deep breath, and declared, "Read on, sir!"

Edward read—page after page of Mr. Mason's sprightly descriptions of the conditions of virtually everyone and everything that comprised Viamede. Old Bess was walking more easily thanks to Dr. Baliss's medications; Veronica had proved to be Mr. Mason's most apt pupil, and she was now helping to teach the little ones to read their Bible verses; young George had been sick with a fever but was recovered, and fortunately it was not contagious; Becca and Thomas had a healthy new son; Mamie was starting her fall cleaning "war or no war"; Marcus was training young Anthony in blacksmithing; one of the spring foals was already showing promise as a runner; Mr. McFee was planning to try a new variety of banana plant in what he called the "experimental" garden; and so on and so on. Mr. Mason's letter, for all its length, was like a healthy tonic, summoning warm images not only of Viamede but of The Oaks and Ion as well. As Edward read, the words flowed over everyone in that London parlor like a warm breeze on a summer's morn in the South, and they could half-see themselves sitting on the verandas or walking the gardens of their homes so far away.

Edward had come to the end of the letter. The last paragraph he read carried great meaning for his wife:

Reports and Regrets

"The arrangements which you made during your last visit are safe with Mr. Mayhew and myself. The papers signed by Mrs. Travilla are locked in the vault at Mr. Mayhew's office, and the second copy is being held by the bank. No one save yourselves and Mr. Mayhew has access to them. Trust me. When the event that you envision comes to pass —as it surely will in God's good time —your orders will be carried out exactly. Whatever the fate of Viamede in this war, freedom will ring."

"May the Lord bless you all."

"What did he mean by 'freedom will ring'?" Trip asked curiously. "What arrangements?"

"Oh, that is just Mr. Mason's exaggerated way of expressing himself," Edward said a little abstractedly. "I simply entrusted him with some business affairs."

Trip shook his head in mystification and said, "He does take his responsibilities seriously, I suppose." Then he went back to playing with Rose and Missy.

Edward looked across the room to his wife. He could almost see the sparkle of satisfaction in Elsie's glistening hazel eyes. She smiled at him, and instinctively he smiled in return. If Trip had been paying close attention, even he might have guessed that some secret had just been exchanged between Mr. and Mrs. Travilla.

CHAPTER

8

Dark Days

"I tell you the truth, whoever hears my word and believes Him who sent me has eternal life. . . he has crossed over from death to life."

JOHN 5:24

Dark Days

The families had been in England for almost six months when Elsie, Edward, and Horace made a journey to see an old friend. They arrived in Edinburgh, the ancient capital city of Scotland, in the early afternoon of a cold and damp November day. After checking into their hotel, they immediately set forth by carriage for the charming stone cottage that they all remembered so well.

Mrs. Katherine Randall met them at the door.

"Come in! Come in!" the handsome young woman exclaimed in delight. "A warm fire, hot tea, and a very excited lady await you in the parlor."

The guests were bustled inside and quickly relieved of their heavy cloaks by Becky, the housemaid and cook.

"It's so good to see you again," Becky said happily. "Mrs. Murray has been looking forward to your visit, and I've been counting the days."

"As have we all," Katherine added. "I only wish today was less gloomy. But I do believe you have brought the sunshine indoors with you."

"How is she?" Elsie asked in a soft tone.

"She is very ill, as you know, and she has grown weaker in recent months," Katherine replied. "But she is not in pain, and I believe you will be surprised when you see her. I cannot explain it very well, but even this great and final challenge does not diminish her. Come now, for we should not keep Aunt Mary waiting one second longer."

Katherine ushered the three new arrivals into the parlor.

Mrs. Murray was sitting in her comfortable old chair before the fireplace. She was small and thin, as she had always been, and she did not rise when they entered but extended both her arms in welcome.

95

Elsie's Troubled Times

Elsie rushed forward, fell kneeling beside the chair, and was enfolded by the gentle arms that had always been open to her in love. Looking on, Edward and Horace saw the glow in Mrs. Murray's face and the mist of happy tears in her eyes. Both men were struck by that face. They knew that her illness was severe, but the woman they saw before them appeared—could it be?—younger than she had at their last visit five years previously. Her hair was no less gray; she had no fewer wrinkles. But something about her seemed to radiate light, as a girl of sixteen seems to glow with life. Perhaps it was only a trick of the firelight, but Horace was especially taken by the sense that the frail old lady before him was unchanged by either age or illness.

After several minutes, Mrs. Murray spoke, "Ach, how good God is to me."

She released her hold on Elsie, who sat back on her heels. The old lady framed Elsie's face with her thin, soft hands and looked into her eyes. "You have altered, my girl. Not in beauty. Oh, no. But I see great happiness in your face. Did I not tell you that an open heart finds its reward?"

Elsie smiled. "You told me, dear Mrs. Murray, and you were right as always. God has blessed me with more love than I had any right to expect. And now He has brought me back to you."

Mrs. Murray held Elsie's face a moment longer, then let her hands slip away.

"Mr. Dinsmore, my old friend. And Mr. Travilla," she said in a surprisingly strong tone. "Come close that I may see you. I fear my eyes are not as sharp as they once were."

The two gentlemen came forward, and Edward assisted Elsie to rise. Behind them, Katherine Randall and Becky were moving chairs forward.

"Please, be seated," Katherine said. "Aunt Mary, will you entertain our guests while Becky and I prepare tea?"

Mrs. Murray smiled, and they all saw the old twinkle. The guests took their seats, Elsie beside her old friend and the two men opposite her. Soon they were eagerly answering her questions about their families both near and far.

Mrs. Murray asked first of Rose.

"This trip has done her good. She is quite well now," Horace said, "and also very sorry that she was unable to accompany us. But she hopes to see you soon, perhaps in the spring. She planned to come with us, but I'm afraid our young Rosie came down with a cold, and you know how mothers are."

"I do," Mrs. Murray said with a gentle laugh. "Now tell me, Elsie, about your babies."

Beaming with pride, Elsie did just that, describing in detail the special charms of her little Missy and Eddie. And this was followed by news of all Mrs. Murray's friends and acquaintances in America.

Tea arrived, and Katherine Randall joined in the discussion. A very happy hour had passed when Mrs. Murray said, "Mr. Travilla, I cannot tell you the sadness I felt upon hearing of your dear mother's death. Sadness tempered by joy for her, that she is now with our Heavenly Father."

Edward nodded and said, "She is truly at home, Mrs. Murray."

"I am reminded of her daily," Mrs. Murray went on. "Do you see this quilt on my lap?"

"I recognized it immediately," he replied, a gentle smile upon his lips.

"I shall never forget the day we opened the trunk your mother sent to me," Mrs. Murray said. "So many treasures, and this exquisite quilt in the last package. The other quilt lies upon my bed, and when I am gone, my dear Kathie and Eliza will receive them, and someday my nieces will pass them on to their children. So even here in Scotland, the memory of your mother's generous spirit and goodness will live on." As she spoke, her hand smoothed the beautifully detailed quilt spread across her knees. "This is how we should be remembered, my dears, by the good works we have done."

Katherine, who was gathering the tea things, said, "Then you will be remembered by many, Aunt Mary, for your good works are legion."

Elsie was astonished by this remark, for its casual reference to death seemed oddly insensitive. Mrs. Murray caught the look on Elsie's face. "Do not be surprised, dear child, if we seem to speak lightly of my dying," the old lady said. "I know that my time here is drawing to an end. But God is kind to me, don't you see? I cannot know the hour of my passing, but He has given me notice that it is approaching. It is up to me how I use this gift, and I have decided to make the most of it. Kathie and Eliza and I—we talk often of life and death now, and of God's wonderful promise. He has given me a good many more than my three score and ten years in this world, and He is even more generous for He has allowed me this time to consider and prepare. I would be an ungrateful child if I wasted His gift with sorrows and fears and regrets, wouldn't I?"

Elsie laid her hand upon Mrs. Murray's. "Forgive me," she said as tears rose in her eyes, "but I can hardly bear thinking of this world without you."

"Nor can we," Kathie said, "but Aunt Mary has always been our best teacher, and now she is teaching us perhaps the hardest lesson of all for humans to face. Death is inevitable, and we must accept that, but it need not be fearsome."

"I am a fortunate woman," Mrs. Murray said. "I think of what is happening in your country today, of the young men preparing themselves for battles in which many lives will be cut short in an instant. I pray for them, my friends, that they will be ready when their time comes."

The room was silent for some moments as each of the guests considered Mrs. Murray's words. Horace moved closer to the fireplace. He broke the silence at last by saying to Katherine,

"We have told you all about ourselves. But what of you ladies and your families? How is Mrs. MacDoogal's son? If I remember correctly, he and my Rosie are of the same age."

"If your daughter is seven now," Katherine said, "then your memory is faultless, Mr. Dinsmore."

Horace laughed, "Ah, if only that were so. But on this point, I have remembered well. Indeed, Rosie is seven."

"Our Robbie, too," Mrs. Murray said, her eyes twinkling, "and more full of energy than a steam engine. But he is not the only one. Eliza and her husband have another son, Andrew, who is three. And Kathie's wee baby girl is but a year. It is another of God's great gifts that I have lived to see a new generation born. Perhaps we shall have all our beautiful children together soon."

The guests and their hostess chatted for a few minutes more, until Katherine whispered to Edward that her aunt was tiring. Politely, Edward indicated that it was time to take leave, but they all promised to return the next day.

As they were about to depart, Mrs. Murray said suddenly, "Is Chloe with you by chance?"

"She is," Elsie replied. "She stayed at the hotel to unpack."

"Then please bid her to come with you tomorrow. You know the value I place on her friendship, and I am anxious to hear about her reunion with her husband and granddaughter."

The guests did return the next day, with Chloe. Was there ever a sweeter meeting than this one?

For a week, Elsie, Edward, Horace, and Chloe made daily appearances in Mrs. Murray's home. Eliza MacDoogal, Mrs. Murray's elder niece, introduced the American visitors to her two sons—robust boys with excellent manners and bright red hair—and Katherine brought her baby daughter one day.

When Elsie worried privately that so much excitement might be too much for her old guardian and teacher, Chloe was reassuring.

Elsie's Troubled Times

"Miss Elsie, you know how that lady is," Chloe said plainly. "She wants to fill her last days with life. This visit with you and the rest of us means a lot to her. Her day of rest is coming soon enough, and that can't be changed. But every minute with her family and friends—why, they're more precious than gold and diamonds. Don't you fret yourself none about tiring her out."

"I wish now that we had brought Missy and Eddie," Elsie said with a little sigh. "I do hope we can return when the weather is a little milder."

"No ma'am, you were right not to travel with those little ones. It's not cold here like it gets up in the North, but this rain and damp would be hard on the babies. But I got an idea."

"What, Aunt Chloe?"

"When we all get back down to London, maybe you could go to one of those photography places and have a picture made of you and the babies. Mrs. Murray has pictures of you. She keeps them in frames in her bedroom, right on the table beside her bed. I reckon she'd love an image of you and Mr. Edward with the children."

"That's a wonderful idea," said Elsie enthusiastically. "We have arranged to have a portrait painted, but a painting cannot be shared like a photograph. Do you think the children will sit for it?"

"I can't say for sure. If you tell Missy how important it is, she'll be still. But little Eddie. That child can wiggle like a worm on a hook. But it's worth trying, don't you think?"

"It most certainly is," Elsie agreed. "I will talk to Edward and arrange a sitting as soon as we are back in London."

Just before Christmas, a package arrived at Mrs. Murray's cottage. Inside was an attractive silver frame containing a photograph—two serious adults, a lovely little girl with curly

locks and large eyes, and a sturdy little boy of two who possessed his father's handsome features. This photograph was given pride of place amid the collection on the table beside Mrs. Murray's bed.

"I hope Mrs. Murray cannot see the grief in our eyes," Elsie had said to Edward on the day the photograph was delivered to them. "I would never have had this picture made did I not think it so important for our old friend."

"I do not believe she will see the sadness," her husband replied. "I fear that grief will be our companion for some time yet. You were right to have this done while she may yet enjoy it."

Providing the photograph for their old friend had been, in truth, an action of sheer willpower for Elsie. Two weeks earlier, the rented townhouse on the pleasant London street had become a house of mourning. On the day after the Travillas and Horace returned from Edinburgh, a large packet of mail—letters, newspapers, magazines from America—was delivered to Quince House, but when its contents were poured upon a table in the library, one envelope caught everyone's attention.

It was a small white envelope, deeply etched about its edges with a border of black. Rose, who stood beside the desk with her husband and Elsie and Edward, gasped at the sight, and Horace instantly put his arm about her waist to steady her.

The envelope was addressed to Rose in May's unmistakable handwriting.

"You must sit down, dearest," Horace said, leading Rose to a couch and taking his place beside her. Then he instructed Elsie to bring him the letter.

"Are you prepared for this, Rose?" Horace asked anxiously. "If so, I think it is best to know the news now."

Rose was deathly pale and trembling, but she looked into her husband's eyes and spoke clearly. "It is the shock of seeing what I have for so long dreaded. But you are right. Will you read it for me?"

Elsie unsealed the envelope and removed the pages. Horace, keeping one arm firmly around his wife, took the pages and scanned them quickly. Then he began to read in a steady, deep voice. May's words came like a physical blow to everyone in the room:

"Rose, Rose, how hard it is to tell you. Our Fred has been killed and Richard wounded—both in the battle for Ball's Bluff on the Potomac. They were both shot while trying to swim the river. Fred's wound was instantly fatal, but Richard swam on to shore, bearing Fred's body, before he collapsed from loss of blood. He was rescued by several of his comrades and taken to a hospital in Washington. They took Fred back as well. When we received the dreadful news, Edward went immediately to Washington to bring Ritchie and Fred home. Fred's funeral was held yesterday. Daniel could not return for it, for he is with the Army in Illinois and was not allowed to take leave. As I am writing this to you, Daisy sits beside me, writing to Sophie, but we have only a small hope that a letter can reach her at Ashlands.

"Dear sister, I do not know how we shall bear this loss. Mamma is heartbroken, and Papa seems almost to have become an old man overnight. The boys fought bravely, dearest Rose, but the odds were overwhelming. The battle was stupid and ill-conceived. Even now, Congress is investigating what went so terribly wrong. But what does it matter? Fred is gone from us forever. Yet we may take comfort in the knowledge that he was ready. Ritchie says that just before they were ordered to retreat across the river, Fred told him, 'We have little chance of making it out of here alive, but if I fall and you live, tell our parents and the others not to grieve for me. I have put my absolute faith in God and entrust myself to His will.'

Hold his message in your heart, dearest Rose, as I do. Fred is in Heaven now where all wounds are washed clean.

"Ritchie is recovering, and he says he will return to his unit as soon as he is well. In his anger and pain, Edward wanted to enlist immediately, but Papa and Adelaide have convinced him that his duty lies here.

"How I wish I could be there with you, for words written on a page like this are cold and stark. But we are all with you in spirit."

"Your loving sister, May"

When Horace finished, no one could find words adequate to express their shock and sorrow. For many minutes, the silence was broken only by Rose's soft sobs. Horace had let the sheets of May's letter drop to the floor as he took Rose in both his arms and rocked her gently.

"Dear, sweet, happy Fred," Rose finally managed to say through her tears. "Never was a boy so cheerful nor a young man so full of love and laughter. I cannot believe I will not again see his bright face in this life."

"Let his own final words console you, dearest," Horace said softly. "Fred is with our Father now, where there is no war or pain."

"I know, I know," she moaned. "I should not grieve, but I cannot help myself. My baby brother. So young. So full of promise."

After some time, Rose had composed herself, but Horace insisted that she go to their room and lie down. After he had escorted her from the library, Elsie and Edward allowed their own sorrow to surface. They sought strength and comfort in one another's embrace.

"When will it all end?" Elsie asked as Edward cradled her head against his shoulder. "How many must die like Fred before this horrible war is done? How many more sisters and mothers and wives must receive letters like that which has brought such sorrow to my Mamma?"

"I have no answer," Edward said, his voice shaking with emotion. "I simply do not know the answer, my beloved. But this grievous loss makes me appreciate all the more what Mrs. Murray said to us. Life is a gift, my dear Elsie, and we must make the most of it while we are here. We must love and care for the living now. We must strive to be good and wise and just. But we must also accept what we cannot understand and not allow our losses to make us bitter or resentful. Remember that whatever happens, it is God's plan, and not ours. With faith, Elsie, this gift of life—however short or long it may be—is only preparation for our eternal life in our Father's many mansions."

9

A Call for Freedom

"The Lord sets prisoners free...
the Lord lifts up those who
are bowed down."

PSALM 146:7, 8

A Call for Freedom

*A*fter the lull that had fallen on both North and South following the Battle of Bull Run—months of anxious anticipation during which the armies of both sides were being transformed from farm boys and store clerks into soldiers—the North began its drive southward in January of 1862. The first battleground was Kentucky, which had reluctantly sided with the Union.

Union troops broke the South's defensive line at a tiny village called Mills Springs on January 16. In February, Ulysses S. Grant led 15,000 Union troops and a flotilla of gunboats called "ironclads" and seized Fort Henry and Fort Donelson on the Cumberland River near the Kentucky-Tennessee border. Meanwhile, more Union forces moved through Missouri and took control of key locations on the Mississippi River. Grant pushed his army deeper into the South, to a place called Pittsburg Landing in Tennessee, just twenty miles from the South's important east-west railway junction at Corinth, Mississippi.

The Confederates, under General Albert Sidney Johnston, had fallen back to Nashville, the capital of Tennessee. Determined to stop the Union's rapid advance, General Johnston and 45,000 Confederates moved southward, and at dawn on April 6, 1862, the Southern forces attacked at a place near a country meetinghouse called Shiloh Church that gave its name to the battle. At first it seemed that the Confederates might triumph. But a Union division positioned in a grove of trees on the bank of the Tennessee River held their ground against wave after wave of attacking Confederates. It was here, at the "Hornet's Nest" as the frustrated Southerners called the place, that General Johnston was shot in the last charge. The Unionists finally surrendered, but their heroic defense had bought time for their comrades. Reinforced by fresh troops,

Elsie's Troubled Times

General Grant attacked the enemy the next morning, and by the end of the second day of fierce and bloody battle, the Southerners were driven into retreat. Their commander was dead. More men had been killed, wounded, or captured at Shiloh — nearly 24,000 in all — than in all prior American wars.

⁓

Newspaper accounts of the battle of Shiloh reached London some weeks later, and reports continued of Union victories. A fleet under David Farragut entered the Mississippi at its mouth and occupied New Orleans at the end of April. The South had lost its largest city and most important seaport. In June, Union and Confederate gunboats met in battle below the bluffs of Memphis, and another Southern city fell. Corinth, Mississippi, with its vital railway lines, was captured by a federal force. The Union seemed poised to take back all of the western portion of the Confederate States. Was it possible that an end to the war was at hand?

Letters from America continued to arrive at Quince House. May Allison was a faithful correspondent. She reported that Richard, who had insisted on returning to his unit as soon as he regained his strength, had fallen ill and was being treated in a Washington hospital, and May had gone to the capital to nurse her brother.

"You will never guess who is his physician!" May wrote in the month which bore her name. *"Your friend Dr. King from Lansdale, who is now an army surgeon. And guess who is here as well. Lottie King whom we all came to love at Elsie's wedding and saw many times while she was teaching in Philadelphia. She is assisting her father now, and I do believe she could be a doctor herself, for she is the most capable and*

compassionate of nurses. She has taken a most particular interest in Ritchie's care, and he is making rapid progress. Dare we think that even in the midst of so much suffering that friendship may yet bloom into affection? At any rate, I was overjoyed to lend my poor skills to Ritchie's care. Lottie taught me a great deal, and I was able to help with other patients as well. Many, like Ritchie, suffer from illnesses, for the conditions in the camps are not favorable to good health. The battles here have been waged by the Navy and the port at Norfolk has been recaptured, but as yet, the worst of the fighting is in the West.

"Daniel has written that he, too, has met an old acquaintance. Phillip Ross, who is the husband of Lucy Carrington, is serving with a New York regiment. Daniel has seen him several times, and Mr. Ross reports that Lucy and their children are fine, and Lucy is busy organizing the women of their community for the war effort. How her heart must break to have her husband and her brother on opposite sides! Though women do not face battle, I am beginning to think that our courage is often of equal measure. To think that when we were all last together—Lucy and Phillip, dearest Sophie and Harry, and so many others—it was on that happiest of days when Elsie and Edward pledged their vows to one another. Would we have been so happy and joyful had we known what awaited us?"

The newspapers brought news of battles and victories. Names like Mechanicsville and Gaines' Mill, Savage Station, and Malvern Hill suddenly became more than mere pinpoints on a map as the Union forces at last made their push to capture the Confederate capital at Richmond, Virginia, only to be repulsed by the forces of Generals Robert E. Lee and "Stonewall" Jackson. With its victories in Virginia, the Confederacy seemed to have turned the tide once more, and like a child's seesaw, power rose first on one side, then on the other.

It was at the beginning of September when a long letter from the Allisons brought unexpected news. Mr. Allison wrote to Rose:

"Dear Daughter,

"We have received word at last from our dear daughter Sophie — her letter brought to us by a freed slave who wandered for many weeks behind the Confederate lines before he was able to escape onto free soil. Sophie is well and at the time she wrote, so was Harry. She did not say where he is serving, but my guess is that he is with Lee's army in Virginia. Though Harry wears the uniform of our enemy in this monumental struggle for democracy and the Union, I shed tears of rejoicing upon hearing that he is alive. I know Harry's cause to be wrong, but he is a man of honor and as good a husband to Sophie as I could want. How could I wish him ill fortune?

"Sophie had other news that has brought tears of sorrow to us all. Both Walter and Arthur Dinsmore have been killed. Walter fell at Shiloh, where Enna's husband, Dick Percival, also met his end. Sophie had no details of their deaths except that they both died in battle. Arthur, who was serving in Virginia, was wounded at Gaines' Mill. Though he somehow managed to return home to Roselands, his wounds became sorely infected, and he died soon after. Mr. and Mrs. Dinsmore are shattered. If only there were some way I could comfort my old friend. Horace Sr. and I have shared much over the years; now we are united in the loss of beloved sons. How I wish that he knew the comforting love of our Lord and could turn to Him in his bereavement.

A Call for Freedom

"Adelaide has taken the news of her brothers very hard but finds consolation in the knowledge that Walter had accepted Jesus Christ as his Lord and Savior. Of Arthur, we will never know if he had opened his heart to Christ, but given the changes he had made in recent years, we can hope that he found faith.

"Rose, you must convey this news to Horace and Elsie. I wish that I could perform this task for you, but I know that you have the strength and love to help them bear their tragedy. Share your burden with Edward Travilla. He is the wisest of friends and counselors."

Mr. Allison's letter went on to tell of everyone in the family. Richard had recovered and returned to his regiment. Daniel had been promoted and now served as an adjutant to General McClellan. Mrs. Allison, May, and Daisy were all involved in war work: May had volunteered to assist a local physician, and both Mrs. Allison and Daisy were engaged in a project to raise money for the widows and children of fallen soldiers. Edward and Mr. Allison himself were kept constantly at the factory where they produced clothing, tents, and other supplies for the Union troops. And Adelaide had begun teaching at a small school for the children of freed and escaped slaves. "Working with mind and hands," Mr. Allison said, "is a balm to the heart. We must grieve, for we are human, but we must go on."

The closing words of his letter were devoted to the progress of the war:

"I fear that our side has lost the initiative. President Lincoln seems to understand the importance of taking swift action, but he is not a military man, and his generals are slow and disunited. It seems that the Confederates, though greatly out-manned by our forces, have brilliance in their generals.

Many here wonder if we have reached a turning point, but I continue to have faith in the President and the Union. Yet we have all learned a lesson since this war began, since Bull Run and Shiloh. Wars are not easily fought, no matter how just the cause. They are not won by waving banners or singing songs, but by the shedding of blood. Was compromise really impossible? Was this war really unavoidable? I do not have the answers, but I sense that we will pay a dreadful price for our divisions and that the payments will be extracted for many generations to come.

"But take no notice of your old Papa's ramblings, dearest Rose. Comfort Horace and Elsie, kiss your children each day for us, and continue writing of the news from England. Your mother and all the family send their love and good wishes. We miss you but are truly grateful that you and the children are safe from harm."

"Your loving father"

Elsie's and Horace's grief when told of the fates of Arthur and Walter was intense. Elsie had always had a special place in her heart for Walter. And for Arthur? She felt his loss all the more keenly because she understood how difficult his struggle had been to turn his life in a new direction. Two young men — the one who had so recently become a Christian, and the other who was striving so desperately to put away his selfishness.

Horace, after the first shock, immediately turned his thoughts to his father.

"Poor, Papa," he said to Rose. "For all his harshness, he loved those boys, and now he is alone. Despite his failings, Papa is a good man, and he always valued the goodness in Walter. And though he was angry with Arthur for so many years, he was strongly supportive of the changes Arthur was making. I know my Papa too well, Rose. He will grieve for Walter and Arthur, but he will not forgive himself for the mistakes he made in rearing them. It is part of his pridefulness. Papa will hold himself at fault for their deaths."

Then Horace cried out, in a tone of such anguish that it almost frightened Rose, "Dear God, please make Yourself known to my poor father! Help him look into his heart and find Your love and forgiveness. Be merciful to him, Lord, in his hour of loss. Let the scales drop from his eyes, and let him accept Your mercy and Your promise of redemption and eternal life!"

Clutching her husband tightly, Rose could say no more than a fervently whispered "Amen."

This outburst gave Horace a much-needed release for his pain, as prayer always gave him relief and hope. So he was well-composed when, a little later that day, he went to Trip's room to break the news. The boy's reaction took the father by surprise.

"I hate this war!" Trip exclaimed in anger. "I don't understand it, and I don't understand why Uncle Walter and Uncle Arthur and Uncle Fred had to die in it!"

Trip stormed across the room and began pacing rapidly back and forth. "I always wanted to be a soldier because I thought it brave and gallant. How stupid of me! My uncles aren't brave and gallant. They are only dead!"

He stopped in his tracks and looked to his father. At sixteen, he was a handsome young man, almost as tall as Horace. But now his face shone with the extreme paleness of one who is wracked with fever. His eyes glowed with a strange wildness.

"Why did God let this happen?" he demanded. "Why, Papa?"

Horace went to his son and put his firm, strong hands on the boy's shoulders. He spoke in a voice that was both certain and kind.

"We cannot know God's purpose, but we cannot doubt Him even though we sometimes suffer from that which we cannot understand. God is not cruel. He loves His children with a love that surpasses our understanding. I cannot tell you, Son, why He has chosen to take your uncles now. But my faith tells me that they have gone to a better place."

Horace felt Trip's shoulders relax a bit under his hands.

"But to die as they must have. In so much pain," the boy said.

"It is terrible for us to contemplate," Horace said softly. "But they died doing what they believed to be right. They were soldiers, my son, and they were brave and gallant. They were also, I believe with all my heart, ready to face God's call when it came. Even poor Arthur."

Horace slipped his arm around Trip's shoulder.

"You would not dishonor your uncles by doubting the faith that sustained them, would you?"

"No, sir," Trip replied as his anger subsided. "I do not doubt my faith. Yet am I wrong to question this war, Papa? Is it not stupid for Christian to fight Christian?"

"Remember that in His plan for us, God gives us choices," Horace said. "War is a choice made by men, and I believe this war is a wrong choice. But it has been made, and we must face it. I do not know when, but the war will end. And when it does, we will need all our faith as we rebuild our beloved nation. We cannot give way to doubt. God will give us the strength if we place our trust in Him. We honor our lost loved ones not by questioning God's purpose, but by remembering their lives and by thanking our Heavenly Father for sharing those lives with us."

As Horace spoke, tears began to fall from Trip's eyes. "I shall miss them very much, Papa," he said with a little sob. "Perhaps Uncle Walter most of all, for I knew him best and he was always so kind to me."

"Then center your thoughts on those good memories," Horace advised. "Remember Walter's kindness and his gentle righteousness. Remember Fred's open nature and loving heart. Remember the courage Arthur showed when he fought off his worst nature and put the needs of others above his own desires. It is human to feel sadness, Trip, and sometimes sadness takes the form of anger. But do not direct your anger at God, for He loves you.

"I once felt anger at the loss of someone I deeply loved. I let my anger feed my pride until it almost overwhelmed me. And it almost led to the destruction of another whose love for me was pure and trusting."

Now Trip was surprised. "When was that, Papa?" he asked.

"Long before you were born, and even before your mother and I had met. It is a story I will tell you someday. But not now, Son. Now we must join the others, for sorrow is upon everyone in this house today. Can you be strong for your mother and Elsie and your sister?"

"I can, Papa," Trip said without hesitation. Then he added, "Thank you, Papa, for talking with me and understanding my thoughts."

"Thank you, my boy," Horace responded, "for sharing your thoughts with me."

Throughout the fall of 1862 and into the winter, the battles raged on. Lee and the Confederates drove the federal forces back to Washington. Though the nation's capital was spared, the armies of the South pushed into Maryland and toward Pennsylvania. At Antietam, men of North and South fought to a bloody stalemate. The South—suffering from lack of fighting men and supplies—suffered another blow when it failed to get official recognition by the British. There would be no help for the embattled Confederacy from outside its borders.

Elsie's Troubled Times

On the first day of the new year, 1863, President Lincoln issued his promised Emancipation Proclamation, declaring that all slaves in areas not under control of the federal government were freed and were "forever free." This document, which was immediately denounced in the South, nevertheless made it clear that no longer was slavery an issue for individual states to decide. At last the words written in the Declaration of Independence, that "all men are created equal," rang true. With the freedom of nearly four million enslaved blacks in the South at stake, compromise was no longer an option.

It was some days later that Edward and Horace first heard the news of Lincoln's Proclamation while they were away from Quince House on business. They hurried home in great excitement and burst into the parlor where their wives were having tea.

"Lincoln has done it," Edward declared. "He has freed all the slaves."

"God be praised!" Rose said.

"What does it mean?" Elsie asked.

"Little, I am afraid, for the war," Edward said honestly. "It may even strengthen resolve in the South, for our neighbors will never submit to the end of slavery. But it strengthens even more the cause of the North, for its soldiers will carry the banner of freedom into battle."

"And what of our homes and our people?" Elsie asked again.

Edward came to the couch where Elsie sat and took his place beside her. "The day we envisioned has arrived, dear wife, and our people are freed. My instructions to our agents were clear. On hearing word that the federal government had declared freedom for the slaves, each person at Ion and Viamede would receive the necessary papers. And each was to receive as well our offer to continue on in our employ. If any choose to leave, they may do so. But even with legal papers, freed slaves will be in great danger now. Lincoln's

A Call for Freedom

Proclamation will appear to the Confederates as a call for a slave rebellion. Mr. Mason at Viamede and my agent at Ion are to make it very clear to the people of each plantation that until the war is over and it is safe to depart, the plantations are havens of freedom."

"As is The Oaks," Horace added, "for the same instructions have been put into action there."

"I do not worry about our security or our ability to pay our workers," Elsie said, "for we have invested wisely. But I admit that I am fearful of what will become of the plantations and our homes. Save for that one message from Sophie, we have heard nothing from the South in almost two years."

In a quiet voice that nevertheless carried great confidence, Rose said, "It is possible that all may be gone when we can make our return. We must face that possibility. But whatever comes, the land will remain, and if we must start from scratch, that is God's will."

Horace could not contain his smile. "And if The Oaks has been reduced to rubble and the fields burned and all the servants have gone? Will you be so eager to begin again, my dear?"

Rose gave him a stern look. She sat very straight in her chair and folded her hands primly in her lap. "I am still young, Husband, despite my gray hairs. And I am strong enough for any task. We have been blessed with prosperity. If God intends us to know poverty now, I will gladly meet the challenge." Then a little smile broke upon her face, "I can cook and wash and sew, and what I cannot do, I will learn."

"I have no doubt of it, dearest," Horace replied. "But I do not think it will be necessary for you to plow or pick the cotton. As Elsie said, we have invested wisely, and though this war will cost us, the price in money will not be so severe as others of our South will suffer. Those whose fortunes are tied only to the land may well lose all."

"Then we must be prepared to be generous with our money," Elsie said with intensity. "We must respond to every worthy cause when we return. Rose is right that we have been blessed. But now we must remember the lesson that Paul taught for the wealthy: 'Command them to do good, to be rich in good deeds, and to be generous and willing to share. In this way they will lay up treasures for themselves as a firm foundation for the coming age, so that they may take hold of the life that is truly life.'"

"You speak wisely, dearest," Edward said, taking her hand. "Wealth is meaningless except as a way to do good for others."

~~~

As the family talked in the parlor, down in the kitchen, a conversation of a very different sort was under way.

Joe could barely contain his excitement. He hopped back and forth from one foot to the other and raised his hands high above his head.

"Thank you, Jesus! Thank you, Lord!" he sang out. "I never thought I'd live to see this day. But You've answered my prayers, Lord, and I can die happy and free."

"What are you going on about, old man?" demanded Chloe, who had entered the room just in time to hear her husband's words.

Joe took her by the arms and danced a little jig. "I'm free, Chloe! And you're free! Mr. Edward told me when he came in the door just now. President Lincoln has freed all the slaves."

At the startled look on Chloe's face, Joe went on, "Believe it, Chloe. Just like God freed the children of Israel from their bondage, He has broken our chains. Free *forever*—that's what Mr. Lincoln said. That means you and me and Dinah and her children and every black child to come. Think of it, Chloe. And bless You, Lord, for Your merciful goodness!"

A Call for Freedom

But Chloe pulled away from Joe's grasp and sank down upon a sturdy chair.

"What's the matter with you?" Joe asked in concern.

Mrs. Dowd, the cook, who had watched the little scene while she stirred a pudding, laid aside her spoon and came to Chloe.

"It's a shock for her, it is," the kindly cook said. "Even good news can be a shock."

Chloe looked up into her husband's face. In a whisper, she asked, "What does this mean for us, Joe? Will we have to go away from here? How will we live?"

"No, old girl, we won't go away. Mr. Edward said that we'll always have a place with the family." He took her trembling hand and began to pat it. "Why, Miss Elsie can't get along without you, Chloe. Not the children either. What it means is that you're a free person now, and there's nobody who can ever buy you or sell you or sell me away like the old master did."

"Are you sure we won't have to leave?" Chloe asked, for in truth Joe's news was only just sinking in.

"Didn't I tell you what Mr. Edward said? And he was grinning like a cat when he told me. Mr. Horace, too," Joe replied. "You just ask Miss Elsie. You and I got places with Miss Elsie and Mr. Edward for as long as we want. We can go or stay as we like because we're free people now."

"It is a wonderful thing," Mrs. Dowd said in a soothing voice. "Course a person's got to work, but it's nice to know that I can take a little holiday every now and then and go down to Exeter to see my daughter and her babies."

"That's it, Chloe," Joe said encouragingly. "It's not what you do that makes you free. It's the knowing you can do it that counts. I guess you and me are a mite old to be going off on our own. But think about Dinah. Now she won't have to hide away the fact that she can read and write as good as anybody. Why, she might get to go to school now, become a teacher like she wants."

"Gracious, that's the truth," said Aunt Chloe. And the more she thought about it, the more this new freedom began to appeal to her.

"Just take some time to get used to the idea, dearie," Mrs. Dowd advised smartly. "Freedom won't make you rich or happy, and it won't mean life is any easier for us poor folk. But it's a wonderful thing nonetheless, to know that you're your own person."

"You said Mr. Lincoln set us free?" Chloe asked her husband.

"He sure did," Joe answered happily. "And now we best hope that the Yankees hurry up and win this war. Then we can go back home and take a big sip from the cup of freedom that Old Abe has set on the table for us! The Lord has brought our people out of the wilderness at last, old girl."

"Praise the Lord," Chloe said with a deep sigh. Then she bowed her head in thanksgiving and reverently repeated the promise of Psalm 146: "'The Lord sets prisoners free.'"

CHAPTER

A Different
Sort of News

*"I will turn their mourning into
gladness; I will give them
comfort and joy instead
of sorrow."*

JEREMIAH 31:13

A Different Sort of News

$\mathcal{E}$lsie knocked upon her husband's dressing room door, and at his reply she entered. Edward was just donning his jacket.

"Have you a few moments to spare before your business appointment?" she asked.

"For you, darling, I have all the time in the world," he replied, coming forward and giving her a warm kiss.

She looked into his dark eyes and smiled happily. "I have news for you."

"More letters from home?" he asked.

"No, but the post has not arrived yet. Perhaps there will be something today. My news is of a personal nature."

"What is it, dear?" Edward asked, a look of concern darkening his handsome features. "Are the children alright?"

"They are fine, dear," she said, laughing lightly, "and I am glad that your first thoughts are for our little ones. My news does have to do with children, though. Of one in particular who will soon be joining our little family. In June, if I am correct."

Edward's expression instantly brightened, and he swept Elsie into his arms and lifted her off the floor.

"I should have guessed," he said as he set her down, "for you have been particularly lovely of late, my beautiful wife. A new baby! You could not have brought better news! To know that a new life is coming—it is a confirmation of God's goodness and mercy to us. We have had far too much of sadness and loss these last few years."

Elsie hugged him close. "I feel that too, my love. This baby is like a little miracle for us, a reminder that even in the midst of tragedy, life continues and God's loving promise to us is constantly renewed."

"June," Edward said softly. "The beginning of summer. It is fitting that this baby will be born in the season when all life is bursting forth. Boy or girl, it will be a welcome addition to our lives."

~~~

The families had planned a second visit to Mrs. Murray in the spring, and fortunately Elsie's physician agreed that the trip would not be dangerous for her. Except for Trip, who was now in his second year at a fine English school for boys, the children were to accompany their parents to Edinburgh, but clearly the most excited was young Missy. The little girl was six, and greatly interested in every new experience.

"Tell me again about Mrs. Murray, Mamma," she asked one afternoon shortly before their scheduled departure. She was in her mother's room as Elsie dressed for dinner.

"Well, she is the kindest of ladies, and she was my very first teacher," Elsie said.

"Because your Mamma had gone to God?"

"That's right, dear. My mamma was in Heaven, but God was so good to me. He gave me Mrs. Murray and Aunt Chloe to take care of me and bring me up in His ways."

"It makes me sad," Missy said.

"What, dear?" Elsie asked, turning to look into her daughter's face, which was so like a little mirror of her own. "Why, what brings that frown to your brow?"

"It's sad that you didn't have a mamma," Missy replied. "Were you a very sad little girl?"

"Well, I missed my mamma. I did not know her, for she died soon after I was born. But from Mrs. Murray and Aunt Chloe, I knew that my mother was a warm and loving person of generous spirit and a naturally giving nature. And she was a true servant of God. I knew that she wanted me to be happy. So even though I felt sadness, I also felt happy that Mamma was in Heaven with our Father where there is no pain or sorrow."

Missy reached a small hand toward the delicate gold chain that encircled her mother's neck.

"May I see her picture?" Missy asked.

Elsie smiled and drew the worn gold locket from her bodice. Carefully, she opened its face to display the lovely miniature inside. Missy gazed at it with a curious expression, although she had seen the painting many times before.

"She is so pretty," the little girl sighed.

"You look very much like her, my pet," Elsie said. Gently she lifted her daughter onto her lap, and they both continued to look at the face in the picture.

"Is she my grandmother even in Heaven?" Missy asked.

"Yes, she is. You are a lucky child, Missy. You have your grandmother Elsie and your grandmother Eugenia in Heaven to watch over you and your Grandma Rose here to love you and care for you every day."

"Am I named for you, Mamma, or my grandmother Elsie?"

"For your grandmother, dearest. In fact, you are named for both my mother and for your father's mother. 'Elsie' for the one and 'Eugenia' for the other. In that way, you carry on the memories of them."

"But everyone calls me Missy. Why?"

Elsie laughed. "That is what your Papa and Aunt Chloe called you when you were born, and we all thought it suited. Somehow 'Elsie Eugenia' seemed too big a name for such a precious little bundle. 'Missy' is your nickname. But would you rather us address you as Elsie or Eugenia or Elsie Eugenia?"

The little girl grew quite thoughtful. She gazed at the miniature for some moments more before closing it. Then she said with grave seriousness, "I want to stay Missy, Mamma, until I'm more grown. Then I know when people are speaking about me and not you. It's not so con . . . con . . ."

"Confusing," Elsie prompted. "I think that is a wise choice for the time being. It might be very confusing for your brother who is just now getting everyone's names straight."

A happy grin came to the child's face, "Eddie is a funny little boy, Mamma. He always makes me laugh. Will the new baby be funny like Eddie?"

"I don't know, pet," Elsie said. "It is one of God's many wonders that every child is unique — special — from the moment it is born. Just as there was never a person quite like you or Eddie, the new baby will have its own character and ways. That is why people are so interesting and why each new person we meet should be valued as special."

"What will Mrs. Murray be like, Mamma?"

"Oh, she is very special, dear. She is old now, and ill, so we must be gentle and on our best behavior when we see her. But she loves children very much. Did you know that after she reared me, she took over the care of her two nieces? You will meet them, too, and their children when we are in Edinburgh."

"Tell me about the children, please, Mamma," Missy begged.

And so Elsie and her daughter chatted on for some time about the upcoming visit. Later that night, when the children had been asleep for several hours and Elsie and Edward were preparing for their own rest, Elsie told her husband of the conversation with their daughter.

"She has decided to remain our 'Missy' for the time. She is such a gentle child but also full of curiosity and the desire to learn new things."

"Then she is like you in character as well as beauty," Edward replied.

"I take that as a high compliment, my love," Elsie said, making a little curtsy. "I believe it is time we gave serious thought to her education. She already reads and is beginning to write. Do you think Papa might include her in his lessons? Since Trip has been going to school here, Papa's only pupil is Rosie. I do not want to impose on him, but Missy could benefit so much from his teaching. What do you think?"

"An excellent idea," Edward replied with enthusiasm. "Horace is a born teacher, and I believe he would welcome a new scholar into his class. I'll speak to him tomorrow if you like."

"Please do, dearest. If he agrees, perhaps she can begin when we return from Scotland."

~⁓~

The visit to Edinburgh was salutary for all. Mrs. Murray had clearly weakened since their last stay and was much more often confined to her bed. But she refused to allow her illness to banish cheerfulness from her home.

"From what the doctors tell us, I don't think she will go on much longer," Becky was saying.

Elsie and Rose had taken a few minutes to speak with the loyal housekeeper alone in the kitchen. At Becky's words, Elsie felt hot tears come to her eyes.

"It will be a sad loss," Rose sighed. "But what of you, Becky? I've never seen so efficient a caretaker, but I know the strain must be hard for you."

"I don't feel it, Miss Rose," Becky answered. "Miss Mary and I've been like two sisters here in this house for a lot of years. I am the servant and she the mistress, but somehow it's always been more like friends, if you know what I mean. So caring for her now is no burden to me. It's what a person does for a friend and a sister. Besides, Kathie and Eliza share a big part of the load, and Mr. Randall and Mr. MacDoogal, too. We'll miss her more than I can say when she's gone, but we're doing all we can to make her last days easy. The work's not so hard, ma'am, when it's for someone you love."

"But what will you do," Elsie asked, "when she . . . when she's—?"

Elsie's Troubled Times

"When she's gone? I'll be staying here, Miss Elsie. Mr. and Mrs. Randall and their baby will be moving here in a couple of weeks. You heard that Mr. Randall is taking a teaching position at the University."

"We did hear."

"Well, they're coming in from the country to live here, and Miss Mary has already given them this house. They want me to stay on. Don't you worry, ladies. Miss Mary will have her family and friends here for as long as she needs us."

"Oh, that is good to know," Rose said.

"Is there anything we can do to help?" Elsie asked.

Becky stepped back from the kitchen table where she had been making sandwiches for tea. She put her hands on her sturdy hips and smiled broadly.

"You've done it already, Miss Elsie," she declared. "You've come back and brought your babies, and Miss Rose has done the same. You've got to see how much happiness that has given to Miss Mary. To see those children playing with her own great-nephews and great-niece—why, that's done more for my lady's heart and spirit than all the medicines her doctors can order. Miss Mary knows she's going on, and she's not afraid. She's got the faith to carry her through. But right now, it just makes her happy to see new life sprouting up all around her. You and your good husbands and your beautiful children being here—that's all the help she needs."

"I only wish we could stay longer," Elsie said. "Becky, will you promise to inform me if you need anything, anything at all?"

"I promise, Miss Elsie, but don't be worrying. You've got your own self to care for now, so that new baby will be as healthy and strong as the others."

A Different Sort of News

The Travillas and the Dinsmores stayed in Edinburgh for more than a week, but as no one—especially not Mrs. Murray—wanted to put added stress on Elsie, the visit came to its end as scheduled.

"Good-bye, my dearest child," Mrs. Murray said in her small voice at her last meeting alone with Elsie. "I doubt we shall be together again, but you must write me as soon as the new bairn arrives. If our Heavenly Father can let me wait until then, it is my last wish to know that you and your wee ones are safe."

"I will write immediately," Elsie promised. She sat in a chair close to Mrs. Murray's bed and was leaning forward to catch her friend's every word.

"And promise me, too, that you will always love that good-looking husband of yours. I can plainly see that you make each other happy. Edward still has the twinkle in his eye, and you fairly glow whenever he walks into the room. But difficult times are coming, child, when you return to America. You must protect him and stand tall beside him."

"But he is my protector," Elsie smiled.

"Aye, but there will be times when you must be every bit as strong and brave as he. Give him your strength as well as your love. I have learned many things in my life, and one is that a woman must sometimes bend like a willow and sometimes stand tall like the oak. Understand the difference. As it says in the Book of Ecclesiastes, 'There is a time for everything, and a season for every activity under heaven.'"

Mrs. Murray reached out her hand, so thin now it felt to Elsie as fragile as an autumn leaf. But the old lady's grip was surprisingly firm and warm. Mrs. Murray spoke hurriedly and with a sense of urgency that fortified her voice: "Your time of greatest trial is coming. You will return to a devastated land. My own Scotland has been a battlefield drenched in the blood of its sons. The South to which you will return will never again be as you knew it. You will have to be strong, my Elsie, for your children and for your husband. I have no wish to frighten you. But when you were a little thing, I warned you never to wander thoughtlessly into danger. Let me do that one last time. The danger now is that you will see only loss and sorrow when you go home. Do not mourn for the past. Let God guide your every step, and do not allow regret or resentment to enter that good and open heart of yours. Do not grieve for what used to be. Be strong, stand with your husband, and together, build a new future for your children and their children."

Exhausted by the passion of her own words, Mrs. Murray seemed to sink into her pillow. Her eyes closed, and her breathing was heavy and slow. Had Elsie not been able to feel the living pulse in the hand she still clasped, she might have feared the worst.

"I will be strong," she whispered, bending close to Mrs. Murray's ear. "I promise. God will be my guide whatever comes. You taught me at your knee to put my trust in Him at all times, dear Mrs. Murray, and I have never had cause to doubt your teaching or His love. I will be strong, because God wants me to be strong."

The face on the pillow moved, and the thin eyelids fluttered open. A weak but beautiful smile came to Mrs. Murray's lips, and in it Elsie caught a glimpse of the strong, healthy woman she had known long ago—the little woman with the will of iron and the faith of solid granite that never cracked or wavered.

"God will guide you, Elsie," Mrs. Murray whispered, "because He loves you. You must go now, lest you miss your train. And I must rest after so long a speech."

Elsie, fearing to tire her friend with any more words, began to rise, but the thin hand gripped hers tightly, holding her at the bedside.

"I love you, Elsie."

"And I love you, Mrs. Murray," Elsie replied, struggling against her tears. "Farewell for now."

The restraining hand dropped away, and the eyelids closed as Mrs. Murray dropped into a peaceful sleep. Elsie kissed the old woman very softly on the cheek and listened for several moments to her soft, steady breathing. Reassured, Elsie walked to the door and left. In the narrow hallway of Mrs. Murray's simple home, she at last let the tears flow. Silently she cried for several minutes, feeling both pain and relief. Then she took a handkerchief from her sleeve, carefully wiped her eyes, adjusted her skirts, and went to join her family.

Tiny Miss Violet Adelaide Travilla arrived on a bright morning early in June, and all of London put on its cleanest and brightest attire to greet her. The city seemed to shine in the early summer sunlight. Flowers in rainbow hues were blooming in every garden and park, and the trees were that wonderfully translucent shade of apple green that would deepen within mere days. The sunlight and summer air drew people out of their homes early for strolls along the freshly swept and washed sidewalks of the neighborhood in which Quince House stood. Their laughter drifted up to the second story and through the open window of the bedroom where Elsie lay in her bed, cradling her newest gift. Edward sat close beside her.

"I know that she is red as a beet and wrinkled as an old shirt," he said, "but to me she is more beautiful than any portrait in the Royal Academy."

"That is because she is the reflection of love," Elsie said, gently stroking her baby's cheek with her fingertip.

"Another new beginning," he whispered to the babe.

"A sign of our Father's love and hope," Elsie added. "Let us pray, Edward dearest, that we may soon take her home to a land where peace has been restored."

And over their infant's head, they did pray words of gratitude and love.

An hour later, little Violet and her mother received their first guests. Edward opened the door, and Horace, who was never quite convinced of his daughter's well-being until he beheld her, entered. He held Missy's hand, and they were followed by Rose, who carried a squirming Eddie. The children had been cautioned to be quiet lest they disturb their mother, but at the sight of Elsie's happy smile, Missy ran forward for her first peek at her new sister. She stared wide-eyed into the blanket.

"Well, pet, what do you think of our Violet?" Elsie asked.

"Well," Missy began slowly, "she is very red."

Edward burst into laughter, and scooped up his first-born for a delighted hug. "I have seen purple violets and white violets and even green violets," he teased. "But who ever heard of a red Violet?"

Missy giggled at the joke, and Eddie, too, began to laugh though he had no idea what was so funny.

"Violet was my mother's name," Horace said. "Violet Eva Stanhope."

"I know, Papa. Though I never knew her, it seemed right to honor her in this way. And dear Aunt Adelaide."

"So now we have two Roses and a Violet," Horace said as he took his first look at the latest of his grandchildren.

"She is very delicate and has lovely features," Rose commented on seeing the babe. She looked up and found Missy's eyes. Then she smiled and said, "She will be another beauty like her sister."

Missy smiled back, a little shyly.

Then Eddie, still held firmly in Rose's arms, piped up, "Can baby play now?"

Another round of joyful laughter filled the room, and Eddie, finding himself the cause of so much jollity, forgot all about the baby.

"I think we best not stay too long, children," Rose said, "for your mamma is tired and needs to rest."

"Yes," Edward agreed. "Missy, take one more look at your baby sister, and then perhaps Rose will allow you to play with Rosie until dinnertime."

Missy, who was in truth awed by this new sibling, came shyly back to the bed and peeped cautiously into the blanket in Elsie's arms.

In a little whisper she asked, "Will she always be so red, Mamma?"

Elsie moved her free arm and drew the little girl close, kissing the top of her curly head. "No, darling Missy," she said. "She will change and grow as quickly as you did, and in not many days, you will see how she has altered."

"Are you very tired, Mamma?" the child asked in concern.

"I am a little tired and very happy. I just need a little rest now, as does our Violet. Will you come back and visit with us after dinner?"

"Oh, yes, Mamma," Missy replied with glee.

Horace took his granddaughter by the hand and said cheerfully, "Come now, young Missy. You and I will find Rosie. I know she wants to hear all about the baby. I think she also has a new book that she would like to show you. It's about a brave boy named Arthur who became king of all England. Would you like to see it?"

Missy beamed as she accompanied her grandfather from the room, followed closely by Rose and Little Eddie.

When they had gone, Elsie turned to Edward. "I will not rest, dearest, until you promise to do something for me immediately," she said firmly.

"Whatever you request."

"First, send Dinah to me. Then go to the library and pen a note to Mrs. Murray. I promised I would tell her as soon as the baby was born, so if you write now, the letter can be dispatched today. Will you do that for me?"

Edward bent down and kissed his wife. "Your wish is my command," he said, and he lingered only long enough to kiss his wife and baby one more time.

Just two weeks after Violet's birth, the Travillas received another of the black-bordered envelopes that had been all too commonplace in their lives. This one arrived from Scotland, however, and was written by Mrs. MacDoogal, informing the families of Mrs. Murray's passing. She had died peacefully in her sleep and had been buried in the graveyard of the old Presbyterian Church where she had worshipped for so many years. "She was so thankful to receive Mr. Travilla's letter and the news of the baby's safe arrival," Eliza MacDoogal had written. "Our last conversation with her was about the children — all the children she loved and cared for during her life. Her final words to Kathie and me that night were, 'God gave me no children, but blessed me with three wonderful daughters. Tell Elsie how much I have loved you all.'"

Elsie was naturally sorrowful, but she remembered all that her dear teacher and friend had taught her, and she discovered that her grief was not so powerful as her joy. Mrs. Murray had led a long and godly life. Now the lady had made her final journey, and Elsie doubted not even for an instant that Mrs. Murray was with God. Elsie recalled the words of King David from Psalm 24: "Who may ascend the hill of the Lord? Who may stand in His holy place? He who has clean hands and a pure heart." And she offered a prayer of thanksgiving, praising God for His mercy and thanking Him for the life of His good and faithful servant, Mary Murray.

CHAPTER

11

Uncertain
Times

*"O Lord, be gracious to us . . .
Be our strength every
morning, our salvation
in time of distress."*

ISAIAH 33:2

Uncertain Times

ife and death and nature's cycles went forward. In July, when baby Violet was but a month old and already growing pink and round, word came from America of the worst fighting yet. The newspapers arrived first. On the first of July, the accounts ran, Union forces had met General Lee's advancing Confederate army near the small town of Gettysburg in Pennsylvania. The fighting had raged for three days, and on the first day, the South seemed poised for victory. But the Union established a strong line of defense and held against the onslaught. The Southerners had made a final, ferocious charge under General George Pickett's command, but they were beaten back. At last the Union had driven the Rebels into retreat.

One day later, the fourth of July, and far to the west, General Grant's troops had captured the port city of Vicksburg, Mississippi—giving the Union control of the entire length of the great Mississippi River. East and west, the Confederate armies were being forced into defensive positions as the Union strategy to recapture the secessionist states gathered steam.

Although the Travillas and the Dinsmores were cheered by the results of Gettysburg, hoping that the Union victory would bring war's end closer, they took no pleasure in the massive loss of life suffered by both sides on those Pennsylvania farmlands.

A long letter soon arrived from May, full of details and some unexpected news.

"To think we were so close to losing our beloved City of Brotherly Love! If the Confederates had been victorious at Gettysburg, no one doubts they would have marched north toward Philadelphia. The Rebels were outnumbered, though the soldiers here in the hospital tell us that they fought like

crazed men. But our army held the line at a place they call Cemetery Ridge. We are only now learning of the extent of the casualties. I have heard numbers as high as 50,000 dead, wounded, or captured on both sides, and some say that General Lee's army was reduced by a third.

"After the last two years of fighting, the best of our Union generals are in command, and the victories at Gettysburg and Vicksburg seem likely to assure the President's re-election. Frequently now, we hear calls for the President to give General Grant control of our armies. Some complain of the general's character, but as Papa says, Grant knows how to be a leader of men.

"It is strange that I can write so easily of warfare, but no one has escaped its influence. You will be surprised, when you return, to see how little sheltered we are. I am helping in the hospital here, and we have recently been joined by Dr. King and dear Lottie. My chores are not easy: I assist with changing dressings and feeding and shaving the patients who cannot care for themselves. The most difficult of my duties, however, is writing letters for our soldiers. I wrote one today for a young soldier blinded by a mortar shell explosion. The letter was to his mother, and I know that she will be overjoyed to receive word of his survival. Yet I could not stop thinking about what the future will hold for him and the others who have received such grievous and maiming wounds. This terrible war will end, but that blind boy will never regain his sight. And what of those who have lost legs and arms, and those once strong young men whose wounds will never heal fully? What is to become of them and their families? And of those whose minds have been shattered by the dreadful sights of the battlefield? Dr. King tells us of the wards at night, when the silence suddenly gives way to screams and sobbing as the wounded re-live the battles in their nightmares.

Uncertain Times

"They say that General Grant will move on Richmond now, but I believe the Rebels will fight for every inch of their ground. Each night I pray that they will come to their senses and that no more lives will be sacrificed to their lost cause. Out-manned, out-gunned, unable to receive but the barest of supplies from abroad—how can the South fight on?

"Yet even in the midst of tragedy there is good news. Daniel has come home! And with him is your cousin from Ohio, Harry Duncan. We had not received any word of Daniel for many months, and only now do we know what he has endured. He was sent on a mission to Tennessee where he was ambushed, struck by a bullet (a flesh wound only), and captured. He was then sent to that abominable prison at Andersonville. It was there that he by chance encountered Harry Duncan. They had never met, you know, but Mr. Duncan happened to overhear a conversation in which the name 'Dinsmore' was mentioned. He inquired and soon learned that the speaker was Daniel. As it turned out, Daniel and several of his comrades were plotting their escape from that dreadful place, and Mr. Duncan joined their plan. I do not know all the details, but they did escape. Though several men were quickly recaptured, Daniel and Mr. Duncan were able to evade the Rebel guards and make their way north. Once they were almost discovered and hid for several days in a swamp. They were pursued by bloodhounds, too, and would surely have been killed had not an old slave found them and shown them how to throw the dogs off the scent by rubbing turpentine upon their feet. They lived on nothing but roots and berries and made their way constantly to the north until they at last came upon an encampment of federals. Mr. Duncan says that they owe their lives to the smell of coffee that guided them through the woods to that camp.

"*They were both taken to a hospital in Washington, and then brought here. With rest and good food, Mr. Duncan has fully recovered now and will soon leave to rejoin his regiment. Daniel has been less fortunate. His wound, though minor, was never treated at Andersonville — Oh, what horror stories we hear of these prisons for the captured! The wound was infected, and Daniel was virtually starved. Mr. Duncan cleaned the wound and kept it dressed as well as he could, and I do believe his attention has saved Daniel's arm. But we do not know. Dr. King says that Daniel is so severely under-nourished that the infection may return. But be assured that our dear brother is receiving the best and most loving of care. You will, I know, include him in your prayers.*

"*We miss you, dear family. And we all await the day when you return. But we take comfort in the knowledge that you and the children are safe. Thank you for the packages of food and medicines you have sent. All have been most welcome at the hospital. God bless you.*"

"*Your loving sister and friend, May*"

At the bottom of the last sheet of her letter, May had written a hasty postscript:

"*I nearly forgot the most exciting news. Our brother Richard is engaged to wed Lottie! As yet Richard has been unable to present her a ring, for jewelry is not easily found in a military camp. But Lottie says that a twist of string is all she needs. So not even war can stay the course of true love! Adieu, my dears.*"

The families were gathered in the parlor when May's letter arrived. Horace had read it aloud, and his reading prompted much lively discussion. But Rose had taken the letter and read

it again, to herself, and when she finished, she pulled Elsie aside.

"Please, Elsie dear, read over what May has written and tell me if you notice anything unusual."

"What should I look for, Mamma?" Elsie asked.

"I shall not tell you," Rose said, and Elsie thought she saw a little sparkle in her mother's eyes. Rose added, "I think I may be seeing what is not real, and I want your objective impression."

Elsie, very curious now, read the letter carefully. Near the end, she began to smile.

"I believe I see the same as you. In at least three instances where May has written 'Mr. Duncan,' she had first written 'Harry' and then scratched through it with her pen. Do you think . . . ?"

"You know how Horace warns us both against matchmaking," Rose whispered confidentially, "but yes. I cannot believe our May, who is always correct in her manners, would take such a liberty if she had not come to know Mr. Duncan very well."

"Perhaps Lottie and Richard are not the only couple for whom love has bloomed," Elsie said with a little giggle.

"We must not jump to conclusions," Rose replied, trying to keep her expression serious. "Yet I seem to remember that Mr. Duncan was most attentive to May when they first met, at your wedding. She was too young for thoughts of marriage then, but now — well, it would be a good match, don't you think?"

Elsie answered with a knowing smile, and the ladies turned to their husbands who were engaged in an intense discussion of General Grant's military strategy. But the news of Lottie King's engagement to Richard Allison and the possibility of romance for May Allison and Harry Duncan lightened their spirits.

Elsie's Troubled Times

For the moment, it appeared that the tide had indeed turned in the terrible war that was tearing the great United States apart. Union victories mounted as the Confederates were pushed back into their own territory. By November of 1863, following General Grant's victories at Lookout Mountain and Missionary Ridge, near Chattanooga, the Rebel forces were forced out of Tennessee and into Georgia. Throughout the Union, there was hope that the war was coming to its close, although no one underestimated the determination of the beleaguered Rebels to resist with force.

The year 1864 dawned with hope, but by the following summer, the outcome was less certain. General Grant was given command of all the Union armies in the early spring of 1864. To General William Tecumseh Sherman, Grant assigned the task of taking Georgia and cutting off the Confederates' remaining supply lines. Grant himself led the Union armies against Lee in Virginia. Again and again the armies clashed, and although the South lacked the strength and resources for victories, they fought on, and the loss of lives on both sides mounted while little progress was made.

By summer, the people of the North were disheartened and war-weary, and even President Lincoln feared that he might lose the next election. His major opponent, General George McClellan, would run for the Democratic Party. The Republicans had split into two factions, the Radicals and the Unionists, and the Radicals were putting forward their own candidate for the presidency.

Tossing his newspaper on the desk one morning in August, Horace declared, "Lincoln needs a decisive victory if he is to win the election and remain as President. Look at this. The Radical Republicans are already planning to take their revenge by crushing the South after the war. They could win the war and then lose the peace by grinding the losers to dust."

"And the Democrats would sue for an immediate settlement which would solve nothing. They would take the nation back to the situation before secession," Edward said in disgust. "It cannot happen. Only President Lincoln can win the war *and* the peace. But something must occur to break this log jam. The people of the North are losing confidence in Lincoln, and their patience is thin. Yet I know his course is right."

The full weight of frustration and anxiety showing in his face, Horace could only sigh dejectedly. He sank into a chair, as if the burden had suddenly become too heavy to bear.

"Should we begin to think of returning?" he asked plaintively.

"Returning to what?" Edward said. "You and I, my friend, are too old to fight, and we will not put Elsie and Rose and the children in harm's way. We do not even know if our homes are still standing. Why, just to go back to the South would be giving moral approval to the causes of slavery and secession."

"And that we cannot do," Horace said.

"No, we cannot. I pray the day will not come when we must separate ourselves from the land of our birth, yet I cannot contemplate returning to a South that is not part of the Union. We must wait, Horace, for the tide to turn decisively. I cannot believe the Confederacy has the strength to hold out much longer."

"And yet they fight to the death for every hillock and inch of ground," Horace said. "You are right, of course. We must wait. But for how long? How long?"

At the very time when Horace and Edward were holding their dispirited conversation in London, a battle was being waged in the waters off the coast of Alabama that would boost the morale of all Unionists. Rear Admiral James Farragut led his fleet into Mobile Bay, sealing off one of the South's last important routes to the sea. On the first day of September in 1864, General Sherman finally occupied Atlanta, and in September and October, another Union army took control of the Shenandoah Valley in Virginia.

With the taste of victory sweet in their mouths, the people of the Union went to the polls in November and re-elected President Lincoln by a clear majority. There would be no change of captain on the mighty ship of state.

Grant in Virginia and Sherman in the Deep South began tightening the noose. Sherman's men marched south across Georgia, cutting a band of destruction designed to destroy the Confederates' richest sources of food and supplies. Just before Christmas, his army seized Savannah, and then it turned north into the Carolinas and toward Virginia. A last, desperate Rebel try for a victory in the western Confederacy had failed at Nashville, and from Tennessee, Union cavalry rode through Alabama and destroyed the last of the South's vital munitions works.

By the first days of 1865, the Confederate States of America comprised little more than parts of the Carolinas and Virginia. Like two arms of a giant fighting machine, the Union armies moved toward Richmond.

In early April, Sherman's army entered Virginia from the south. And on April 2, Grant's forces broke General Robert E. Lee's Army of Northern Virginia at Petersburg, which was the gateway to Richmond. What remained of the government of the Confederacy fled their fallen capital just in advance of the victorious Unionists. President Lincoln himself came to Richmond and walked its streets where he was greeted by a joyous throng of former slaves.

The end came a week later when, on April 9, 1865, General Lee offered his sword and surrendered his battered army to General Grant. The terms of the surrender were generous. The defeated Confederates would be given food and allowed to return to their homes on the promise that they would not renew the fighting. They would not, Grant pledged, be punished for their rebellion. When the victorious Union troops began firing their cannons in celebration, Grant ordered that they stop. The soldiers of the South had fought long and bravely, and their defeat was not a cause for glee and gloating. "The rebels are our countrymen again," he was reported to say.

The war was over. The nation would be one again. But at what terrible costs no one as yet could imagine.

Five days later, on the evening of April 14, President Abraham Lincoln was shot and killed by an actor and Southern sympathizer named John Wilkes Booth in Washington's Ford's Theater. "Father Abraham," who had freed the slaves and presided over the restoration of the Union, was dead. At the moment when he was most needed to lead his country into peace, the captain had been cut down by an assassin's bullet.

CHAPTER

12

Reunions

"How good and pleasant it is when brothers live together in unity!"

PSALM 133:1

Reunions

On the bank of the sparkling creek, a girl of about eight dangled her bare feet in the cool water. She was reading a picture book and seemed hardly conscious of the sights and sounds of summer that surrounded her. She wore a simple calico dress and a bright, white pinafore. In the afternoon light of the sun, her dark curly hair seemed touched with gold.

A boy of six played happily near the stream, gathering sticks and large, flat leaves which he fashioned into little boats to sail upon the shallow stream. He was perhaps a bit taller than most children his age, a handsome boy who talked as he worked: "Put your backs to it, boys! We sail at dawn!"

As their mother watched her children, a picture came to her mind of another curly-haired little girl with her feet in the stream and a book in her lap; of a lively blonde girl building fairy castles of leaves, sticks, bits of bark, and moss; of a fun-loving boy sailing his fleet of leaf boats on the water.

To Elsie, it seemed that time stood still in this place. She might have been ten years old again, playing with Sophie and Daniel Allison beside this meandering creek at the bottom of the meadow at Elmgrove. What had been the names of those two nice schoolgirls who had invited them on the strawberry-picking expedition? As Elsie's memory went back over the years to those carefree days of her childhood, she could almost believe that there had never been a war and that everyone she loved was safe and well. If only it were so.

The Travillas and the Dinsmores had been back in their native land for just a few days. They had accepted the invitation of the Allisons to stay at Elmgrove for the summer; they would make their way home when the weather began to change and the danger of fever in the South had passed. In fact, the Travillas were staying in the new house that Edward and Adelaide Allison had built next to her parents' summer residence. Horace and Rose were with Rose's mother and father in the old place. They were not the only ones gathered at Elmgrove. Both houses and the quiet country setting of Elmgrove served as haven now for the wounded, the homeless, and the bereaved.

As soon as the peace had been made, Sophie Carrington Allison traveled from Ashlands with her children and her mother-in-law, Mrs. Carrington. Sophie's husband, Harry Carrington—the gallant friend of Elsie's youth—had fallen in Pickett's Charge on the last day of battle at Gettysburg. Old Mr. Carrington, that jovial man who had always been so indulgent with the children, had died of a fever which swept his plantation in the summer before the war's end.

How sad Elsie and Sophie's reunion was. Elsie hardly recognized the woman in her widow's clothing. The change in Sophie was heartbreaking. The cheerful little girl, always so full of chatter and fun, was gone—replaced by a thin and drawn woman whose large eyes had turned dull with sorrow. Sophie almost never smiled except when her children were present, and even then her expression was but a ghostly remnant of her once glowing happiness.

Stealing some time from the others on her first evening at Elmgrove, Elsie had joined her friend in Sophie's old bedroom—its cheerful yellow decor contrasting dramatically with the young widow's black gown and cap of mourning, her pale complexion and haunted eyes.

"It is the strangest thing, Elsie," Sophie said in a flat, emotionless tone, "but I can no longer cry. When I first received the news of Harry, I could not stop weeping. There seemed no end to my well of tears. Yet this is worse. I think of him at all times.

I see his face before me when I am awake, and I dream of him in the few hours when I can sleep. I have heard stories of the men who lost arms or legs in battle. They say they can still feel the limb long after it is gone. That is how I feel, dear friend, as if Harry were still with me. There are times when I think I am mad. I sense him standing behind me, about to grasp my elbow as he so often did. Yet he is not there. If I turn around, I will see nothing."

Elsie did not know what to say. Her friend's grief was so bleak.

"God will comfort you," Elsie managed at last.

"Oh, He does," Sophie declared, and Elsie was greatly relieved to hear the emotion in Sophie's voice as she spoke. "Do not fear, Elsie. I have not lost my faith. God is my rock and my salvation, and His purpose for me seems clear. I have four wonderful children to bring up in His way. Harry loved our little ones so much, you know. I think there was never a man like Harry. So full of life and love."

The two friends sat side-by-side on Sophie's bed, and Elsie wrapped her arm about her friend's tiny waist.

"He loves you still, and someday, you will meet again and be together for eternity," Elsie said softly.

"I know. I do believe that with all my heart and soul," Sophie replied. She was looking down at her hands, at the golden band on her left ring finger. "For the children's sake and for Harry's memory, I am trying very hard not to become bitter. But I cannot escape this feeling that a part of me is missing."

She turned her face suddenly to look into her friend's eyes. "People like to say that time will heal this feeling. I want to believe that, Elsie. I really do. But I am so afraid that I will forget Harry."

"God will heal you and protect your memory," Elsie said firmly. "You must trust our Lord completely. He will gladly bear your grief, Sophie, just as He bears our sins. Think of the sacrifice He made for us on the cross. Remember His pain. And now He shares your pain. Open your heart to Him. Hold back nothing. And He will give you His healing love."

"Am I being very selfish, Elsie, in my sorrow?" Sophie demanded, grasping Elsie's hand with surprising strength.

Elsie thought carefully before she spoke. "I believe that grief is natural," she said slowly, "that it is part of God's plan. It can be selfish, though, if we allow grief to overwhelm us and shut down our capacity for love. Think of the love that you and Harry shared. It hasn't died, Sophie. It lives on in your children and in your heart. God wants us to grieve, but He doesn't want us to turn our backs on life. He wants us to grow in wisdom. If you cannot let go of your grief, then you cannot grow as God intends for you. I think you may be afraid to give up your grief because it seems that you will be giving up your love for Harry. But that's not true, Sophie. Harry lives on in your heart. But if you allow your sorrow to harden your heart . . . . "

Sophie interrupted, "Then I will destroy the very thing I value most, the love that Harry and I shared. Oh, Elsie, thank you so much for speaking plainly to me. No one else does. Even Mamma and Papa seem afraid to hurt my feelings by talking forthrightly."

"Your parents have suffered more than their share of loss, and if they are fearful of hurting your feelings, it is from their concern for you. They do not want to add to your sorrow."

"But in my sorrow, I am adding to theirs," Sophie said with conviction. "I have much to think about. May we talk of this again, Elsie? I know you are willing, but I fear that my conversation has become awfully depressing."

"You can never depress me," Elsie laughed, and Sophie's face broke into a genuine smile.

"There it is!" Elsie exclaimed.

"What?"

Reunions

"The smile that Harry loved so much. I thought perhaps you had banished it from your face."

A warm blush suffused Sophie's cheeks, and with it came the youthfulness that had always been so much a part of her.

"Do you think a smile is perhaps a greater tribute to my beloved husband than these widow's clothes?" she asked a little shyly.

Elsie hugged her tightly and replied, "Harry loved you in all your moods, dearest. Yet I think he would be proud to see you smile again. And I do look forward to more of our talks. I remember once when I was depressed and confused, at the time of your wedding. You did not fail to speak plainly to me then. You must let me return the favor now."

There were plenty of hours for Sophie to talk with her good friend. Sophie and Mrs. Carrington planned to remain with the Allisons for some time, for they no longer had a livable home. Ashlands, their plantation in the South, had been ransacked and partially burned in the last days of the war; the house still stood, but it was a mere shell. The fields had lain barren for several years, and there was very little money left and no men to see to the rebuilding. Lucy Carrington Ross and her children were coming from their home in New York to be with her mother and Sophie. Lucy's husband, Phillip, had survived the war without injury, and he would join the family in another week or so. Together, the family had many decisions to make.

Daniel Allison was also at Elmgrove where it was hoped that the fresh, country air and good food would aid his recovery. In truth, Daniel's health had been broken by his long confinement in the Confederate prison at Andersonville. His wound—if only it had been treated properly at the time—might have healed easily, but without medical attention, it had become a constant source of infection and pain. Worse was the terrible damage caused by months of near-starvation and polluted water in prison. It was clear to all that Daniel would have died at Andersonville if he had not escaped and been brought north by Harry Duncan. Even now, the doctors held little hope for Daniel's survival, for despite all their efforts, the young man only weakened. Daniel appeared resigned to his fate.

"Do not look so sad, Elsie. My hope is with Him who gave His life that we might have eternal life," Daniel had said to Elsie on their first private visit. He was in his bedroom, sitting in a wheelchair, and she had brought him a large bouquet of flowers fresh from the garden. Though the day was warm, Daniel was wearing a shawl about his shoulders and a blanket covered his legs. He was clearly ill and very frail, but a light seemed to shine in his face, and his eyes were bright and young.

"I want to live," he went on. "Believe me, I do want to live. But I am ready for whatever comes. If God calls me home to Heaven, I will obey His command gladly."

"But you must not give up hope," Elsie replied desperately.

"Don't you see that hope is my strongest ally?" Daniel responded. "Hope of eternal rest in the house of my Heavenly Father. But I do not want to dwell on what may come. I understand now that each new day is a gift to be savored and appreciated. Now, tell me of yourself and your family. You have three beautiful children, I hear."

So Elsie told him about her little ones, and Daniel seemed to take genuine pleasure in her descriptions of Missy, Eddie, and little Violet and their activities.

"I hope you do not mind," she concluded, "but we have taught them to call you 'Uncle Daniel.'"

"Mind? I am thrilled, and I look forward to meeting my new nephew and nieces. But answer me this, Elsie. Are you as happy as you appear? Does Mr. Travilla treat you well?"

Reunions

Elsie laughed and replied, "I am exceedingly happy, and yes, my husband treats me well if by that you mean he loves and respects me and protects me and our children."

"Ah, then, I shall not have to challenge him," Daniel smiled. "There was a time when I considered doing just that. My illness has one compensation, Elsie. It somehow forces me to be honest."

Elsie, who had not intended to bring up the subject of Daniel's letter to her, sensed that he wanted to discuss his feelings.

"When you wrote to me, I was honored by your confession," she said a little tentatively.

"I hoped that letter would not cause you pain, but I wanted you to understand the cause of my long absence. When I realized that my love for you could never be returned, I was distraught and not altogether rational. In my despair, I accepted my employer's offer to go to Central America, but my time there was curative, and eventually I understood that even unrequited love has its purpose. God had given me a choice. I could allow my disappointment to turn to bitterness, or I could accept my loss. I discovered that bitterness is a most unsatisfactory companion."

Then he told her something of his life in Central America and the many interesting people he had met there.

"Do you realize, Elsie, that God gives us opportunities wherever we are? Even prison was part of His plan for me and the others. Will you go to my dresser?" he asked.

Elsie rose and walked to the large chest at the opposite side of the room.

"Do you see there a little package in brown paper?" Daniel asked.

Elsie's gaze immediately fell on a small, rectangular bundle wrapped in worn and dirt-stained paper and tied with frayed twine. She picked it up.

"That is for you, Elsie. Let me tell you the story before you open it."

She came back to her seat at his side and held the package as he spoke.

"I do believe that God puts us where we need to be," Daniel began. "When I first arrived at Andersonville, many months before I encountered Mr. Duncan, I met a guard, a young Rebel who had fought at Shiloh. We talked and soon learned that we shared our faith although we fought on opposite sides. He was kind to me, and when he could, he provided me with an extra portion of food or fresh water. We talked often of our families and our homes before the war. At some point I mentioned that my sister was married to Mr. Dinsmore of The Oaks plantation. The young guard was very surprised by the name. 'Is this Mr. Dinsmore by any chance related to a Walter Dinsmore, a lawyer?' he asked me. 'Walter Dinsmore is his brother,' I replied, 'and yes, he was a lawyer before the war. I know him well.'

"It developed that the guard had served in Walter's unit at Shiloh, and they were friends. I had not then heard of Walter's death, and it was the guard's sad duty to tell me of his fall in battle. Then the guard asked an even more astonishing question: 'Do you know a girl whose name is Elizabeth or Eliza?' I inquired if he meant 'Elsie,' and he confirmed that was the name, if Elsie was the niece of Walter Dinsmore."

Daniel halted his narration for a few moments while he sipped from a glass of water.

"You need not go on now if you are tired," Elsie said.

But Daniel was determined to continue. He placed the water glass back on its tray, adjusted the blanket on his lap, and drew in a deep breath.

"There is not much left to tell, " he said. "It was about a week after we discovered our mutual connection to Walter that the guard brought me this." He pointed at the little package in Elsie's hands.

Reunions

"He told me that before the second day of fighting at Shiloh, Walter had entrusted these items to him. They were for his niece, Elsie, should Walter not survive the battle. When the guard learned that Walter, indeed, had been killed, he wrapped the items in the paper you see and put the package among his own things. The man was later assigned to guard duty at the prison, and he almost forgot the little package until the day we talked about Walter. And so he passed Walter's gift on to me, and I carried it in my pocket from that moment on. Now I give it to you."

Elsie was astounded by Daniel's story. To think how far this little packet—this message from her good and noble uncle—had traveled amazed her and touched her deeply.

"Will you open it now?" Daniel asked. "I am only the messenger, but I would greatly like to know the contents."

"Of course," Elsie said as she slipped the twine off the bundle and pulled away the worn brown paper. Inside were three things: a photograph of Elsie herself in her wedding dress, a photograph of Walter in his military uniform, and a small black book. Upon the book, in letters of gold, was written *Holy Bible*.

Tears sprang to Elsie's eyes as she stared at the picture of Walter. "How handsome he is," she said with a small sob.

After some moments, she opened the little Bible, and inside its cover she found a hastily penned note:

"If God is willing, you will never receive this," Walter had written, *"and I will live to see you and all whom I love again. Yet if it is His will to take me, I want you to have my most treasured possession. Read the passage I have marked in the Gospel of John, and be assured that whatever fate awaits me, I meet it trusting absolutely God's everlasting love and forgiveness."*

"Your Uncle Walter"

157

Elsie turned immediately to a place marked in the book by a thin blue ribbon. She saw there a verse carefully underlined in red pencil—John 3:16: "For God so loved the world that He gave His one and only Son, that whoever believes in Him shall not perish but have eternal life."

With a sigh, she handed the note and the book to Daniel. She looked again at the photograph.

"Early in the war," she said, "Walter wrote to me that he had accepted our Lord in his heart and found the love that surpasses all understanding. Oh, sweet, kind Walter. You are at peace now."

"He was a good man," Daniel agreed. "I do not think that, aside from you, anyone in his family really understood him. He did not wear his pride and strength so openly as the others, and his thoughtfulness appeared to some as weakness."

Daniel let his head drop backward against his chair and stared dreamily toward the ceiling. A gentle smile softened his face. "I like to think," he said, "that God calls us home when we are needed there. He needed Walter's generous heart and shy courage, and Walter is now cherished in Heaven as he never was in this life. Walter is happy now. Of that I am certain."

Elsie looked at Daniel's shining face and understood that he spoke as much of himself as of Walter.

"You are tired, Daniel, and I must go," she said. "May we talk more later?"

"I want to very much," he said lowering his face to look into her eyes. "This evening, bring Mr. Travilla and the children, if you please."

"I will, and thank you, dear friend, for bringing these home to me," she said, clutching the little Bible and the photograph of Walter.

When Elsie had gone, Daniel realized that she had left behind the photograph of herself. He picked up the picture from the table where she had left it. For a long time he gazed at the face in the picture — the beautiful face framed in white silk and orange blossoms. Then he slipped the picture into the breast pocket of his jacket, over his heart.

The Travillas and Dinsmores were anxious for any word of the South and their homes, but they were unprepared for the extent of the bad news. Edward Allison had journeyed to the South soon after the war ended, and he reported in detail on the suffering he encountered there.

After word of the deaths of Walter and Arthur reached Roselands, Mrs. Dinsmore had suffered a severe heart attack and died just a month later. Soon after her mother's death, Enna — the widow of Dick Percival — had married a Confederate soldier, but he had been killed in one of the late battles in Virginia. Though not yet thirty, Enna was now a widow twice over. Lora Dinsmore Howard's losses were no less tragic. Her husband, Charles, survived but had lost his arm, and her eldest son had been killed defending Vicksburg. Louise Dinsmore Conley was a widow as well, for her husband had died at Lookout Mountain.

Roselands was destroyed, and old Horace Dinsmore, Sr., was living at The Oaks, as were Enna and Louise Conley and their children.

"Your father is heartbroken," Edward Allison told Horace, "but he knows that he is welcome in your home. He longs to see you and Rose and the children, but he insists that you not return until September when the fever season has passed."

"But I must go now, " Horace protested.

"No, you must not," Edward Allison declared firmly. "Heed your father's warnings. The conditions for travel are very dangerous at present. I had planned to go farther south but decided against it. Your family members are safe at The Oaks, and fortunately your home was not damaged. I believe it has saved your father's sanity to run the place. Your manager was drafted into the Confederate army a year before war's end and has not been heard from. But Mr. Dinsmore has taken charge, and though I cannot explain their loyalty, most of the former slaves remain on the place as employees. After some argument, your father accepted the money I offered him to pay the workers. But he is still a stubborn man and would only take the money if I signed a loan contract."

"Roselands is gone then?" Horace asked.

"The house, yes, burned to the ground," Edward Allison said sadly. "I am sorry, my friend."

"What of Ion?" Edward Travilla asked. "We have heard nothing of its fate."

"I was not able to visit your home, for it was necessary that I cut my trip short and I spent my time entirely with Mr. Dinsmore. I was told that the house still stands, though damaged. But again, the workers have mostly remained, and Mr. Dinsmore said that your manager was determined to plant at least some fields this summer."

"Fever or no fever," Edward Travilla said, "one of us must go south now to ascertain the damage. There is much we can do if we know what is needed. Besides, once at Ion, I may be able to get word of Viamede. I will speak to Elsie first, and with her agreement, I shall leave as soon as possible."

"But —" Edward Allison began.

"I am decided," Edward Travilla said. "We spent the war in safety in order that we might be ready to rebuild in peace. It cannot be delayed. Too many people — free people now — depend upon immediate action."

"Then I must go with you," Horace said, but Edward would not have it.

Reunions

"You have to stay here, Horace, with the families. Think of Rose and Elsie and the children. They need their husband and father and grandfather."

"Adelaide, too," Edward Allison said. "You are the only brother she has now, Horace, and I can see the happiness she feels that you are here for awhile. I can use your help as well, for my work at the factory goes on whatever the season, and I cannot be available to my family during the days."

"And there is one happy event on the near horizon that you do not want to miss," Edward Travilla added. "Harry Duncan will arrive next week for his marriage to May. Stay, my friend, and let me take care of this business."

Though he was not satisfied to remain behind, Horace saw the wisdom of the advice from the two Edwards. And so he agreed to remain at Elmgrove.

Edward bade Elsie and the children farewell two days later. He had planned to travel alone, but at the last minute Old Joe requested permission to join him.

"I don't know what we'll find down there," the old man said, "but I'm mighty anxious to get a look at home again. I've waited more than seventy years for the day when I could be a free man in the South. 'Sides, I can be a help to you, Mr. Edward. You can use an extra pair of eyes and ears."

"We must travel the entire way on horseback, Joe, and I do not know what kind of accommodations we will find on the way," Edward warned. "It will not be an easy journey."

"I don't 'spect it will, sir, but I had about as much luxury as I can tolerate over in London. I got mighty soft over there. I need to toughen up now for the work ahead."

Edward could not restrain a smile at the old man's determination. "Then I am persuaded," he said. "But Aunt Chloe will miss you."

Elsie's Troubled Times

Joe laughed. "And I will miss her, but no more than you will be missing Miss Elsie," he said slyly.

And so the two men departed for the South, and Edward could not escape the feeling that they were traveling to a country that would be more foreign than any he had ever visited.

The women were gathered in the sewing room several days after Edward's departure. They were busy sewing clothing and linens for May's trousseau.

"I wish we could give May a wedding like yours, dear," Mrs. Allison said to Rose, "but that would be inappropriate in these difficult times."

"May has made it clear that she really does not want a large wedding, Mamma, and what you have planned will be lovely," Rose said. "May will have her family and her closest friends here with her. She wants no more."

"At least she will marry in a white dress as you girls did," Mrs. Allison continued. "Do you know that she wanted to marry in her traveling outfit because it was more suitable, she said, to these somber times? But our Daniel intervened. He said that we have had enough of mourning blacks and that she must wear white satin and orange blossoms in her hair. Thankfully, he was most convincing, and May will wed in the most beautiful white gown and veil."

"She will also have this fine trousseau," Adelaide remarked as she finished the last stitch on a monogrammed sheet. "It always amazes me how comforting these domestic duties are in times of trouble. I sew as my mother sewed and my grandmother and her mother. Through war and sorrow, women's work always goes on."

"I am only sorry that Miss Stanhope cannot be with us," Mrs. Allison said.

"At least May and Harry will be going directly to Lansdale after the wedding," Elsie said. "Aunt Wealthy is sure to entertain them royally when they arrive. Oh, I had forgotten to ask. Who will serve as Harry's best man? Is he bringing a friend from Ohio?"

"No, dear, he has asked Daniel. My poor boy is very excited," Mrs. Allison said happily.

"And Richard and Lottie are coming to be with us," Adelaide said happily. "We have not seen them in so long. You know that we were unable to attend their wedding, for the war still raged when they exchanged their vows. But Lottie writes regularly, and she is very happy with her new life as a wife."

"Is she still teaching?" Elsie asked.

"As a married woman, she cannot," Rose replied. "I do think some reform must be made in that regard. It seems a great waste to me that a woman with Lottie's education and abilities should be denied the right to teach only because she has married."

"Why, Rose dear," Adelaide declared in mock surprise. "That remark sounds positively revolutionary. Next you will be saying that women should have the vote."

"I am not a revolutionary," Rose replied nicely, "but I am not blind to the need for change in some things."

"I think Lottie would rather be a physician than a teacher," said Daisy, the Allisons' youngest child who had grown into a lovely young lady. Daisy had thus far been silent as she listened to the older women's conversation.

"What an impossible idea!" her mother gasped.

"No, Mamma, I mean it," Daisy said earnestly. "I saw Lottie work with her father in the hospital. She was extraordinary. She could stitch wounds, and she assisted Dr. King with his surgeries. And she could diagnose fevers and illnesses as well as any of the doctors."

"But that is not proper work for a lady," Mrs. Allison said firmly.

"Who is to say that it is not proper?" Daisy replied in a polite tone, for her intention was not to aggravate her mother. "It is just that I believe there are men alive today in large measure because of Lottie's knowledge and care. As Rose said, it just seems a waste that someone like Lottie cannot be a doctor or a teacher or whatever she likes simply because she is female."

"Well, she is now my son's wife, and that is work enough for any woman," Mrs. Allison said with a laugh.

"It is an interesting idea, however," Rose commented thoughtfully. "I sometimes wonder what the world will be like when our children are grown."

"I wonder that as well," said Adelaide softly, thinking of her own sweet youngsters. "The war has changed us all, and we are only beginning to see the extent of the change. Our beautiful South will certainly never be the same."

"Let us all pray that it will be a better place," Elsie said. "I thank God every day that our glorious Union has been restored. But there is much work to be done if all the wounds of war are to be healed."

CHAPTER

13

A Time To Mend

*"And the God of all grace, who called
you to His eternal glory in Christ,
after you have suffered a little
while, will Himself restore you
and make you strong, firm
and steadfast."*

1 PETER 5:10

*E*dward returned from the South about a week after the wedding of May and Harry Duncan. His report was in some respects most difficult for Elsie, Horace, and Rose to hear.

The country around the estates had not seen battle, but indeed the beautiful old house at Roselands had been destroyed. A unit of Sherman's advancing army had come through the area and ridden first up to Roselands demanding food, water, and other supplies. Old Mr. Dinsmore was inclined to facilitate them, believing that the unit had no intention to loot. But before he could speak to the commander, Enna, who had just two days before received notification of her second husband's death, stormed from the house in a fury of anger and grief. She was waving one of Mr. Dinsmore's antique pistols and gave full vent to her feelings in the most violent and abusive language. Assuming that she spoke for the household, the officer in command ordered that she be restrained and the house ransacked. What happened after that was something of a mystery. Having taken what they needed, the soldiers released Enna and galloped away. But within a very few minutes of their leaving, smoke began to billow throughout the house. The sitting room downstairs and an upstairs bedroom had been set alight, though no orders to burn the place had been issued by the Union commander.

"So it is Enna who caused this outrage!" Horace exclaimed.

"Do not be too harsh in judging her," Edward replied. "While her words may have caused some soldier to commit a rogue act, we do not know it for certain. But your father says that as soon as the fires were discovered, Enna ran up the stairs through smoke so thick it was like night, gathered her and Louise's children from the nursery, and brought them out to safety. Louise herself tried to organize a bucket brigade to douse the fire, but there were so few servants left at Roselands that the task was impossible. The house and everything in it were destroyed, but praise God no lives were lost. The stables remain, as do some of the outbuildings and the servants' quarters. The fire did not spread to the fields."

"Can Roselands be rebuilt?" Elsie asked.

"With enough money," Edward said. "The problem is that Mr. Dinsmore had invested all his fortune in Confederate bonds which are now worth less than the paper they were printed on. The last of the servants fled after the fire, so all he has left are the land and some horses and mules. Mr. Dinsmore might get a small loan on his own, but I doubt it, for his age makes him a poor risk. And he is too proud. He absolutely refuses to approach a bank with his hat in his hands."

"But we have money!" Elsie declared. "More than enough. Even if I have lost every piece of my Louisiana properties, my fortune alone is enough to rebuild Roselands many times over."

She stood up and went to her father. "I want the money used to repair and renew," she said firmly, "beginning with Roselands. It was your home, and mine, and now it is Grandpa's only legacy. You must convince Grandpa to take the money, Papa."

"His pride is so strong," Horace replied, shaking his head. "I know he will not accept a gift of money from you or me, dear Elsie."

"But he might accept a loan," Rose said.

"He might, indeed," Edward agreed, "if it were presented with a clear contract."

"He need not even know it is my money," Elsie added, "for it is really not *my* money after all, but only entrusted to me to be put to good purpose."

"That's true, Daughter, but my father must not be kept in the dark about the source of any loan. For all his faults, my

father is a man who prizes the truth. We would do him a great disservice to withhold any information, even for his own good."

Elsie dropped her head. "You're right, Papa, of course. I just cannot bear the thought of his forfeiting Roselands from misguided pride."

"We may convince him yet," Horace said hopefully. "But Edward, tell us now of The Oaks and Ion."

"The Oaks is in very fine shape, only a little worse for wear. Apparently it was never visited by either army. Some of the fields are overgrown, but the gardens are productive and a new cotton crop is growing. Ion was less fortunate. It was visited by the same federal unit that apparently set fire to Roselands. They did not destroy the house, but they can fairly be said to have plundered it. The only things of value they did not take were my mother's silver service and tea things, which one of the servants hid under his bed in his cabin, and several trunks of her handmade linens that were in the attic. But the orchards and food gardens are intact and productive. My manager somehow scrounged seeds in the spring, and several of the fields are planted. My optimistic estimate is that within six months, The Oaks will be returned to its full glory, and in perhaps a year, we may say the same of Ion."

"Oh, what of your beautiful hothouse, darling?" Elsie asked anxiously.

Edward laughed. "I shall have to take up a new hobby, dearest, for the time being—the fitting of glass windows. The soldiers seemingly took their revenge in the shattering of glass, and not a pane remains. But that is easily remedied. We may even have orchids for your hair by next spring.

"As for our neighbors," Edward continued, "the walls of Ashlands stand but that is all. I will make a full report to the Rosses and the Carringtons, for they must decide whether to rebuild or to sell the place. The Howards' plantation was spared but with Charles so severely wounded and the servants gone, no production is possible. Mr. and Mrs. Howard are in poor health, but Louise and Carrie carry on as best they can, and with the greatest fortitude. I saw Dr. Barton, and he has aged greatly. He is a man whose career has been dedicated to the preservation of life, and the war has worn him down. He carries on, though, and his buggy is seen traveling the roads day and night.

"I went into the city only once and saw more destruction there than in the countryside. The blockade took a terrible toll, and without productive employment, the poverty is extreme in many areas. The harbor was shelled, and the rail tracks torn out. The city fathers are struggling to replace the basic facilities, but they can do little without money for materials and men. I have no doubt that if Lincoln had lived, the rebuilding would be well underway by now, but there are many in the government who want only to punish the South for insurrection. President Johnson is a Southerner, and I know he wants a healing reconstruction, but I doubt he can accomplish much against those who are bent on having their vengeance."

"You paint a dark picture," Rose said with sadness.

"But not so dark," Edward said, "that it is hopeless. Far from it. Ion and The Oaks stand. The land is fertile and will bloom again. And I received news of Viamede. A letter arrived addressed to you and me, Elsie, and I took the liberty of opening it outside your presence."

"What is mine is yours," Elsie said with a little blush. "But who was it from?"

"Our Mr. Mason," Edward replied as he drew an envelope from his pocket. "I might give you the gist of it, but I cannot hope to reproduce his words. Would you read it aloud, dearest, so that all may share his message?"

He handed the envelope to his wife, and she hurriedly removed the thick wad of folded sheets. Noting that the letter dated from late April, she began to read:

"Dear Mr. and Mrs. Travilla,

"I write to you from New Orleans where I have been living for the last year. Believe me I did not leave Viamede willingly, but it became clear that I was about to be drafted to fight in the Army of the Confederacy, and that I could not do for I honor our Father's commandment not to take life. So I volunteered to serve as a chaplain to the Confederate wounded and captured who were held here. It proved to be a most satisfactory ministry, but as our soldiers are now returning to their homes, I will no longer be needed and plan to return to Viamede in another week or so. I hope that our old arrangement will go on as before, but I will understand if you no longer require my services. Your first concern, of course, must be the state of Viamede, and I am most pleased to report that it is nearly untouched by the war and was never visited by either Federals or Confederates. The estate house is unscathed, but there have been so many deprivations that it has suffered from unavoidable neglect. Aunt Mamie and her staff are as dedicated as ever, and the house is always spotlessly clean, but a coat of paint would not be amiss. (Until I left, I personally saw to the care of your most voluminous library.)

"All but a few of the servants remained when they received their emancipation — What a glorious day of celebration and hymn-singing that was! — and of those that left, a dozen or so young men who hoped to fight on the Union side may yet return if they have survived; they made it plain to me that they bore no grudge against their former owners. Mr. McFee, the new overseer, is as capable as we all hoped, and he has kept the plantation running to this day. But there is more good news. Mr. Spriggs was stationed in Mobile after the seizure of that port city, and he has written to me that he would very much like to return to Viamede when he is released from the Union army. (The story of how he acquired my address is quite interesting but lengthy, and I shall therefore reserve it for another time.) I saw Mr. McFee in New Orleans not long after receiving Mr. Spriggs's letter, and Mr. McFee declared that he thought Spriggs's proposal a worthy one. I believe that his age has finally caught up with Mr. McFee; though he makes no complaint, I could see that he was tired and not averse to giving up his heavy load of responsibility. He did say that he and his good wife would be happy to stay on at Viamede, if such is your desire, and to work for Mr. Spriggs.

"As you can see, there are important decisions to be made which explains why I hope this letter will reach you soon. When you consider my own position, you must know that I will not return to Viamede alone. I am now a married man. The Lord God said in the Book of Genesis, 'It is not good for the man to be alone,' and in His infinite goodness, He has provided for me a wife who is in all ways loving and tender and kind. Need I add that she is a Christian of the purest heart? My good wife, who was introduced to me by her father, a fellow clergyman, was a teacher before our marriage in March, and as she has a most felicitous way with children, I thought perhaps she might assist me with the education of the people of Viamede, if this suits your plans. Your people there, who are now your employees, clamor to learn now that the legal barriers have been destroyed, and teaching, which was limited to the children before the war, may now include all.

"I am posting this letter to Ion on the assumption that you and your children will have returned to your home or be there soon. Whatever your decisions regarding the issues I have *raised, please know that I appreciate my past experience at Viamede and my association with your families.*

"May God be with you all,"

"Mr. Mason"

Elsie finished reading and took a deep breath. "My, he does love words!" she laughed.

"Perhaps his new wife is reticent and therefore a good balance has been struck," Edward said with a wry smile.

"Well, it is good to have his words about Viamede, however long," Horace commented. "Have you received any correspondence from the agents in New Orleans?"

"No, but I wrote them as soon as we returned," Edward replied. "Perhaps they have written to us at Ion, and a letter is there now."

"We shall know soon enough," said Rose. "Though I shall miss my parents and Daniel and the others greatly, I am anxious to return to our home and get on with the necessary work."

"We leave in just three days, my dearest," Horace said, taking her hand, "and what a caravan we shall make. Carriages and carts and horses for so many. I fear it will be a tiring trip for you."

"Dear husband," she replied fondly, "my name is Rose, but you know I am no fragile flower."

"No, my dear," he smiled. "Not fragile, and not thorny either."

Edward was fatigued after his long ride, and he retired early that night. After she had seen to the children's prayers and tucked them safely in bed, Elsie tiptoed quietly into her room, taking care not to wake her husband. But Edward was not asleep. Hearing her soft footsteps, he sat up in the bed and turned to adjust the wick of the oil lamp at his bedside. Light flooded his face.

"I thought you would be sleeping," Elsie said.

"I was only resting," he responded. "I must admit that seeing Ion and The Oaks again has made me most anxious for our permanent return. But, my love, there is much work ahead of us. And I want you to know that we need not undertake it if you would prefer to stay here. We have the children to consider, and perhaps it would be best for them to remain in the North."

"Do you really want to stay here?" she asked in astonishment.

"No, but I also do not want to pressure you to return."

"Oh, dearest Edward, you are so sweet and considerate. But I have never had a thought other than returning to our beloved South. How could we abandon her now, when she is most in need?"

"Then you must be prepared. The work ahead of us will be arduous, and there are people who will not welcome our arrival—people who resent that we lived in comfort while they endured all the deprivations of war."

"I do know that, Edward, and I even understand such resentment. But we are strong, and we will deal with whatever comes our way."

"Are you sure?"

"Edward, you have not until tonight doubted my strength or my desire to go back to Ion," Elsie said with firmness. "I have been your wife long enough to know when you are troubled. Did something happen during your trip that has worried you?"

"Not exactly, dearest, but I must admit I was not ready for the extent of the damage I encountered. But what concerns me, Elsie, is something I suspect but have not been told. I believe you may have news that affects us both."

For a long moment, Elsie could only stare at her husband in bewilderment. Then a smile of comprehension came to her face.

"How did you know?" she asked. "I have only just confirmed it myself."

Edward extended his hand and gestured for her to come to his side. Elsie sat down on the edge of the bed.

Edward took her hand and raised it to his lips. Then he said, "You did not marry an unobservant man, my dear. We have been at this place three times in the past, with the most wonderful results. I have learned to recognize the signs. The sweet softness of your expression, the lightness in your step, the particular tenderness with which you indulge the children. Do my eyes and instincts deceive me?"

Elsie's answering smile told him that he was not deceived. "You are correct, my love. You are to be a father again, in about six months. Does the prospect please you?"

"Please me?" he declared. "Nothing could please me more. But you must now understand my concerns about your well-being. I worry about taking you back to Ion and all the work required to revive it. I worry that I cannot devote my time to you as I can if we stay in the North for another year. I worry—"

She stopped his speaking by putting her hand to his lips.

"If my well-being is your concern, then you may stop worrying at this instant," she said. "I am not ill, dearest. Far from it. The prospect of returning home and having this new baby there is exhilarating. Does it not occur to you that God is blessing us in this way for a purpose? It is as if He were saying to us that we are living in a time of new beginnings. So many lives have been lost and damaged by the war. But in peace, life will go forward, and so shall we."

She let her caressing hand drift to his cheek. "Oh, my darling, this new life is like a sign," she went on. "Like the rainbow God set in the clouds as the sign of His covenant with all the generations of mankind. A new baby is God's gift to us and His promise that life will continue. To think of His goodness to us lifts my heart and strengthens my soul. We will rebuild our home and our lives not for ourselves but for our children. I want our baby to be born at Ion. I want all our children to be part of this renewal."

"I warn you, dear, it will not be easy," Edward said.

"No, it won't. But don't we owe it to our children to show them life's problems as well as its pleasures? Should we not face our future together, as a family?"

"Yes, we should," he replied confidently. "I only wanted to be assured that the choice was yours as well as mine. As I missed our prayers with the children tonight, might we have our devotion together now?"

Elsie rose and went to get her Bible from her night table.

"Which passage would you like us to read?" she asked.

"Well, dearest Elsie, it seems appropriate that we consider God's promise in the ninth chapter of Genesis."

Opening the Holy Scriptures, Elsie quickly found the place and began to read: "Then God blessed Noah and his sons, saying to them, 'Be fruitful and increase in number and fill the earth.'"

Her lovely, low voice filled the words with her own hope and joy. With God in her heart and Edward and the children beside her, Elsie knew that whatever adversities lay ahead, her family was ready to meet the challenges. With enormous gratitude to her Heavenly Father, she read the final verses of the passage Edward had chosen: "'Whenever the rainbow appears in the clouds, I will see it and remember the everlasting covenant between God and all living creatures of every kind on the earth.' So God said to Noah, 'This is the sign of the covenant I have established between me and all life on the earth.'"

When she finished, Elsie closed the book and laid it aside. Then she took her husband's strong hands in both of hers.

"In three days, we begin our journey home," she said. "Let us pray for the courage to face our future with fortitude and for the wisdom to greet difficulties with love and understanding. Let us pray for all whom we love here and there. And let us express our thankfulness for the Lord's great blessings — for Missy and Eddie and Violet and the new baby. Will you say the words, dearest?"

"Gladly," Edward replied, and they both bowed their heads as he began to pray.

As Elsie and her family begin to rebuild their life in the South, what enemies, old and new, will threaten their home and happiness?

Elsie's story continues in:

ELSIE'S TENDER MERCIES

Book Seven of the
*Elsie Dinsmore:
A Life of Faith* Series

Collect all of our Elsie Dinsmore books and companion products!

Elsie Dinsmore: A Life of Faith

Book One — Elsie's Endless Wait ....ISBN 1-928749-01-1
Book Two — Elsie's Impossible Choice ....ISBN 1-928749-02-X
Book Three — Elsie's New Life ....ISBN 1-928749-03-8
Book Four — Elsie's Stolen Heart ....ISBN 1-928749-04-6
Book Five — Elsie's True Love ....ISBN 1-928749-05-4
Book Six — Elsie's Troubled Times....................ISBN 1-928749-06-2
Elsie's Christmas Party..ISBN 1-928749-52-6

Watch for these upcoming Elsie titles available Spring 2001:

Book Seven — Elsie's Tender Mercies....................ISBN 1-928749-07-0
Book Eight — Elsie's Great Hope ....ISBN 1-928749-08-9
Elsie's Daily Diary ....ISBN 1-928749-50-X
Elsie's Life Lessons, Vol. I....................................ISBN 1-928749-51-8

And many more to follow!

For information about Elsie Dinsmore and her faith, visit our Web Site at:

www.Elsie–Dinsmore.com

Mission City Press, Inc. • P.O. Box 681913 • Franklin, TN 37068-1913

Check out
www.Elsie–Dinsmore.com

- Get news about Elsie

- Join The Elsie Club

- Find out more about the 19th Century world Elsie lives in

- Learn to live a life of faith like Elsie

- Learn how Elsie overcomes the difficulties we all face in life

- Find out about Elsie products

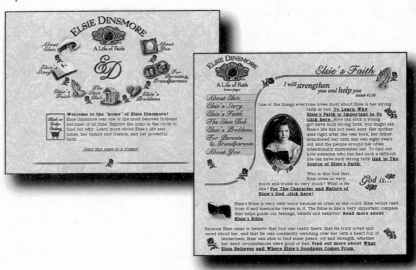

Elsie Dinsmore: A Life of Faith
"It's Like Having a Best Friend From Another Time"

— ABOUT THE AUTHOR —

*M*artha Finley was born on April 26, 1828, in Chillicothe, Ohio. Her mother died when Martha was quite young, and James Finley, her father, soon remarried. Martha's stepmother, Mary Finley, was a kind and caring woman who always nurtured Martha's desire to learn and supported her ambition to become a writer.

James Finley, a doctor and devout Christian, moved his family to South Bend, Indiana, in the mid-1830s. It was a large family: Martha had three older sisters and a younger brother who were eventually joined by two half-sisters and a half-brother. The Finleys were of Scotch-Irish heritage, with deep roots in the Presbyterian Church. Martha's grandfather, Samuel Finley, served in the Revolutionary War and the War of 1812 and was a personal friend of President George Washington. A great-uncle, also named Samuel Finley, had served as president of Princeton Theological Seminary in New Jersey.

Martha was well-educated for a girl of her times and spent a year at a boarding school in Philadelphia. After her father's death in 1851, she began her teaching career in Indiana. She later lived with an elder sister in New York City, where Martha continued teaching and began writing stories for Sunday school children. She then joined her widowed stepmother in Philadelphia, where her early stories were first published by the Presbyterian Publication Board. She lived and taught for two years at a private academy in Phoenixville, Pennsylvania — until the school was closed in 1860, just before the outbreak of the War Between the States.

Determined to become a full-time writer, Martha returned to Philadelphia. Even though she sold several stories (some written under the pen name of "Martha Farquharson"), her first efforts at novel-writing were not successful. But during a period of recuperation from a fall, she crafted the basics of a book that would make her one of the country's best known and most beloved novelists.

Three years after Martha began writing *Elsie Dinsmore*, the story of the lonely little Southern girl was accepted by the New York firm of Dodd Mead. The publishers divided the original manuscript into two complete books; they also honored Martha's request that pansies (flowers, Martha explained, that symbolized "thoughts of you") be printed on the books' covers. Released in 1868, *Elsie Dinsmore* became the publisher's best-selling book that year, launching a series that sold millions of copies at home and abroad.

The Elsie stories eventually expanded to twenty-eight volumes and included the lives of Elsie's children and grandchildren. Miss Finley published her final Elsie novel in 1905. Four years later, she died less than three months before her eighty-second birthday. She is buried in Elkton, Maryland, where she lived for more than thirty years in the house she built with proceeds from her writing career. Her large estate, carefully managed by her youngest brother, Charles, was left to family members and charities.

Martha Finley was a remarkable woman who lived a quiet Christian life; yet through her many writings, she affected the lives of several generations of Americans for the better. She never married, never had children, yet she left behind a unique legacy of faith.